WINNER

Kathy Lee

Each *Seasiders* story is complete in itself – but if you enjoy this book, you may like to read the others in the series:

Runners

Liar

Joker

The same people (plus some new ones!) appear in all the books.

Scripture Union

Will a person gain anything if he wins the whole world but is himself lost or defeated?
(Luke 9 verse 25, from the *Good News Bible*)

© Kathy Lee 2000
First Published 2000

Scripture Union, 207–209 Queensway, Bletchley, Milton Keynes
MK2 2EB, England

ISBN 1 85999 359 1

British Library Cataloguing-in-Publication Data.
A catalogue record of this book is available from the British
Library.

Printed and bound in Great Britain by Cox & Wyman Ltd,
Reading.

Contents

Chapter 1

Don't worry, Darling

Not long after my parents went abroad, I realised I'd made a dreadful mistake.

It was bad enough saying goodbye, knowing that I wouldn't see them again for months. Dad's boss had sent him to the Far East for a year, and Mum was going too.

"Why can't I come?" I had asked them lots of times. The answer was always the same.

"You can't possibly miss a whole year of school, Alexa."

"But there must be schools in Japan and Indonesia and Singapore," I argued.

"Of course there are. The problem is, we'll be travelling around so much," said Mum. "It would be terribly disruptive, darling. You'd be far better off at boarding school in England."

How could she say that? She knew how much I hated the idea of boarding school. Up till then, she had hated it too. She had been on my side whenever Dad suggested that it was time I went away to school. "Oh, James. But she's still so young," Mum had been saying ever since I was eight. I was her only child, and she didn't want to be parted from me.

But now I was nearly twelve, and even Mum had begun to tell me that I was quite old enough to go away to school.

"I don't *want* to," I said. "I'll absolutely hate it – I just know I will. You know Susannah Mills? She hated it so much, she ran away."

Mum looked worried then, but Dad said, "I think you're being very silly, Alexa. How can you know you'll hate a thing before you've even tried it?"

When I was younger, I would have had a temper tantrum at that point. But now I was older and wiser.

"I suppose it might, just might be okay," I said. "But what if it isn't? I'll be stuck there, twenty-four hours a day, seven days a week. Like being in prison. And you won't be able to help me because you'll be thousands of miles away."

I knew what that would do to Mum. She was already feeling guilty about leaving me.

"Why can't I stay on here, at home?" I pleaded. "Marie could look after me." (Marie was our au pair.)

"Marie is going back to France to start her college course," said Dad.

Mum said, "Perhaps you could stay with one of your friends, Alexa."

"For a whole year? That's asking rather a lot," Dad grunted.

He was right. A sleepover was one thing – staying for a year was quite another. I couldn't think of a single person who would be liveable with for a year. Well, there was one, my ex-best-friend Claudia. But we had quarrelled the previous term. (She got into the tennis team and I didn't, even though I was miles better than her.)

Mum said to Dad, "There's always your mother, James."

"Oh yes! I could live at Grandmother's!" I said excitedly. "Great idea, Mum."

My grandmother lived in a seaside town called Westhaven. Every summer I went to stay with her for a week. It was quite fun, although Westhaven wasn't exactly the Cote d'Azur, and Grandmother could be quite strict. (She used to be a school Head before she retired.)

Dad said, "Don't you think she has enough on her plate already?"

I knew what he meant by that. Grandmother already looked after my cousin Edward. His parents had split up years ago, when he was about six. His father went off to live in Australia, and his mother – my Aunt Susan – married someone else. Grandmother had offered to take care of Edward "until things settle down", but somehow, six years later, Edward was still there.

He was a strange boy. I didn't like him very much. Sometimes he was there when I went to visit Grandmother; sometimes he was off in Birmingham, at his mother's. I preferred it when he wasn't there.

Mum said to me, "How do you think you and Edward would get on, darling? It would be for a whole year, remember, not just a week."

"Oh, it wouldn't be a problem," I said airily. "He is a bit odd, but he's never there much. He goes out bird-watching, or shuts himself up in that room that he calls his lab. I don't know what he does in there – probably nothing at all, but he likes people to think he's a sci-entific genius."

Mum said, "I wonder what the schools are like in Westhaven. And of course we'd have to find you a good music teacher..."

"Aren't you forgetting something?" said Dad. "We don't know if my mother would be prepared to put up with Alexa for a year."

"Ask her, Dad. Oh please... I'd much rather stay with Grandmother than go away to school."

That's what I mean about a dreadful mistake.

Grandmother said yes. Soon it was all arranged; I would stay with her in Westhaven, and go as a day girl to the *Barcliff Academy for Girls*. It was in a town about five miles away.

"How will I get to school?" I asked. "Grandmother doesn't have a car."

Mum said, "There are trains. It will be worth the journey, darling. Barcliff has an excellent reputation, much better than any school in Westhaven."

"Is that what Grandmother says?"

"Well... no. Your grandmother actually thought you would be better off going to the same school as Edward – the local comprehensive."

I made a face. "I don't want to go to school with oiks like Edward. Do you know what his friends call him? Neddy. It makes him sound like a donkey."

"Don't worry, darling. I'm sure you'll meet some really nice people at Barcliff," said Mum.

Oh yes? That was another big mistake. But none of us knew it at the time.

My parents took me to Westhaven, along with a carload of my belongings. I wished I could have taken my piano (a baby grand, rather a nice one), but Dad said no.

"There's a perfectly good piano at your grandmother's house."

"It is *not* perfectly good. It hasn't been tuned in years, and half the notes stick."

"In that case we'll arrange to have it tuned," said Dad. "Now don't forget, your grandmother can't afford extra expense like that, so don't ask her. Let us know, and we'll send the money. And your pocket money will be paid into your bank account each month. If you find you need more, just tell us."

"Write every week, won't you?" said Mum. "And of course we'll phone you as often as we can. And you can fly out to meet us for Christmas. I wonder what Christmas will be like in Singapore?"

She sounded excited. I felt left out again. It wasn't fair. Why were they going, and leaving me behind?

"It will be ages till Christmas," I said mournfully. "It's only September now. I won't see you for months and months."

"Oh, darling…" She hugged me tightly. I had made her feel guilty again – good.

"I'm going to miss you so much," she said. "But the weeks will simply fly past. I'm sure you'll have a lovely time at Grandmother's. After all, that's where you wanted to be."

Oh, absolutely.

Chapter 2

Fountain Square

Grandmother lives in the part of Westhaven they call the New Town, although it's actually about 200 years old. The street is called Fountain Square – and yes, you guessed it: there's no fountain. (There is this headless thing, green with mould and white with bird mess, in the middle of the Square, but it hasn't given out any water for years.)

Grandmother's house is tall and thin. The windows are tall and thin and stiff to open. The furniture is tall and thin and old, with sharp edges and awkward corners. And Grandmother fits this pattern too.

She is tall and thin and old and rather stiff. Not stiff in body – at least, not bad for a 68-year-old; she can walk for miles without getting tired. Stiff in manner is what I mean, and in the way she speaks. And she has sharp edges, too.

Always, before, I had slept in the big bedroom on the first floor. This time Grandmother led me up another flight of stairs, and showed me into a smaller room at the back of the house.

"I thought I would be having my usual room," I said, disappointed. "Can't I sleep there, Grandmother?

Please?"

"I like to keep that as the guest bedroom," said Grandmother firmly. "You slept there before because you *were* a guest. But now that you're one of the family, so to speak, this will be more suitable. You can make this room your own, and I won't have to move you out if I have visitors."

"Oh." I gave her the look that works so well on Mum. (Terribly disappointed, but trying hard not to make a fuss.)

Grandmother didn't seem to notice. "And that brings me to something else. While you're here, Alexa, I feel it's only fair that you help with the housework. You must keep your own room clean, and help with the washing-up."

"Washing-up!" I said in dismay. "But I don't know how. We've always had a dishwasher."

"Then it's time you learned," said Grandmother briskly.

I was already beginning to regret my decision. If I had gone to boarding school, I wouldn't have had to wash up. They had kitchen staff to do that.

As for cleaning my room, I vaguely knew how to use a vacuum cleaner. I had seen the au pair do it. But what about all the other mysterious tasks – dusting and polishing, doing the laundry, making the bed? Would Grandmother expect me to change my own sheets and pick up my own dirty socks? I shuddered.

Grandmother said, "Edward always helps with the housework, so it's only fair that you do, too. I shall try to treat you both alike – no favouritism."

I could see it was useless to argue. Head teachers, even retired ones, don't have much patience with argumentative people. A better plan would be to wash up so badly – chipped plates, dirty knives and smeared glasses – that Grandmother would make Edward do it instead.

I could hear his footsteps on the stairs. "Edward!" Grandmother called. "Your cousin's arrived. Come and say hello."

Edward looked in. "Hello, Alexa," he said obediently.

I hadn't seen him for over a year, but he hadn't changed much. He still had fiery red hair which needed cutting, and thick glasses that made his eyes look large and round, like an owl's. I was pleased to find that, although he was six months older than me, I had caught up with him in height.

"Did you have a good journey?" he asked, because that was the sort of politeness Grandmother expected.

"Not bad, thanks. A bit of a traffic jam at Reading."

An awkward silence fell. It's not as if we were friends. We had nothing at all in common, apart from the same grandmother. I didn't like him much; he didn't like me much. Why should we have anything to say to each other?

"Well, I expect you want to unpack your things, Alexa," said Grandmother. "Do come down whenever you're ready. We shall eat at seven." (And don't be late, was the silent order.)

Instead of unpacking, I went to the window and stared out, feeling depressed. The view was not inspiring: roofs, chimney pots, fire escape ladders and rusty pipes. Have you ever noticed that most streets are much nastier-looking at the back? The front is all neat and nicely painted. The back is a mess.

I wished I was in the guest room, looking out on the trees of Fountain Square. Or even better, at home in my own bedroom with its view of smooth lawns and peaceful river. Or best of all, looking down from a plane heading eastward. Oh, why couldn't they take me with them?

I rubbed my eyes fiercely. My parents were gone; it was no good getting upset. What would Grandmother think if she saw I'd been crying? I was nearly twelve. Too old to cry.

Combing my long black hair, I looked at myself in the mirror. Most people think I look older than twelve. Sometimes they ask where I get my exotic looks from – my great-grandmother was Chinese. I rather enjoy being that little bit different from everyone else: unusual, unforgettable.

A sound from outside caught my attention. Below me was Grandmother's back garden, a small square of grass which never got much sun because of the tall buildings. To the right lay two more gardens, and then the back yard of a shop, or café, or something. It was a scruffy-looking place, with overflowing dustbins and piled-up crates of empty bottles.

A boy was down there in the yard. But what on earth was he doing? He seemed to be filling bottles with water from an outside tap. They looked like the kind of bottles that mineral water is sold in.

Surely not! Surely the café wasn't selling "mineral water" that was really tap water? Mineral water was quite expensive – tap water cost nothing at all. The café could make a nice little profit from that.

The boy, who looked about twelve or thirteen, was carefully screwing the top on each bottle, then putting it on a tray. Suddenly, as if he could feel he was being watched, he glanced up at my window. He looked surprised. Then he grinned a cheeky grin, and winked at me.

I found myself smiling back at him. He wasn't bad-looking, with curly black hair, dark eyes, and that grin which seemed to say, "Okay, so you caught me out. But who cares?"

He filled the last bottle. Then, with a casual wave, he picked up the tray and carried it indoors. I waited, hoping he would come out again, but he didn't.

It crossed my mind that if I was here for a year, I might make some new friends. In the past, staying for just a week, I had never met anyone of my own age. (Except Edward, of course, but he didn't count.)

When we sat down to eat, I asked Edward about the boy from the café.

"That would be Darren Wheeler," he said. "He's in my year at school. His parents own the café."

"Rather a down-at-heel place, that café," said Grandmother. "It was quite nice in the old days. Two elderly sisters ran it; they used to bake all their own cakes and scones. Then they retired, and the Wheelers took over. The place has gone steadily downhill ever since."

"Is Darren a friend of yours?" I asked Edward later. He was washing the dishes, I was drying them.

"Well… yes and no."

"What do you mean?"

Edward said, "He's all right sometimes. When he's on his own, I mean. But when he hangs around with Macaulay Burton and his gang, he can be a real pain. They were the ones who started calling me Neddy –

because they knew I didn't like it."

"Why don't you like it?" I said innocently.

"It sounds like a donkey. But I'm stuck with it now. Everyone calls me Neddy, even some of the teachers."

At once I decided that I would do the same. Anything to annoy Edward – I mean Neddy.

"Has anyone ever called *you* a name you didn't like?" he asked me.

"Of course not," I said. "If they tried, I soon put a stop to it. You have to be tough with people – not let them walk all over you."

No one was watching me, so I carefully dropped a plate on the floor. It smashed into a dozen pieces.

Grandmother came rushing in. "Oh, I'm sorry," I said. "It just seemed to slip out of my hand. I hope it wasn't one of your favourite ones?"

Chapter 3

Barcliff

I had never gone to school on a train before. I always went by car with Mum or the au pair. (That is, if the au pair was one who could be trusted with the car keys. Over the years we've had some weird and wonderful au pair girls, such as Helga, who kept forgetting that in England we drive on the left. After she went round a roundabout anti-clockwise, Dad said enough was enough.)

Grandmother said she would come with me on my first day. I didn't really want her to. What would my new schoolmates think – that I was scared to go alone?

But if Grandmother had made up her mind to do something, it was hard to persuade her not to. She marched me down to the station in plenty of time for the train. I saw a few other girls wearing the Barcliff uniform, a rather old-fashioned grey blazer and kilt. Perhaps I would have gone over to talk to them if Grandmother hadn't been there.

The train chugged slowly out of Westhaven station and rumbled over the long viaduct across the river. On the far side, the ground began to rise. Soon we were travelling along a cliff-top – or that was what it felt like. I suppose the railway line was about two hundred metres from the edge. Far below lay the sea, sparkling in the autumn sunlight.

Grandmother pointed out various places of interest. Of interest to her, I mean. Personally I couldn't care less about the nesting habits of seabirds, or the fossils that had been found in the rocks. That was the sort of stuff Neddy liked.

"And this is Sheepstone village, or what's left of it," she said. She pointed to a row of cottages between the railway line and the edge of the cliff.

"Not much of a village," I said.

"It used to be quite a sizeable place, two hundred years ago. There's a painting of it in Westhaven Museum, showing a church, a manor house, and many more cottages. But they all ended up in the sea."

"What?" She had my attention now, all right. "Was it an earthquake?"

She said, "I don't mean it happened overnight. Year by year, the sea ate away at the coastline. Every time there was a bad storm, a bit more of the cliff face crumbled away. Houses had to be abandoned when they became too dangerous to live in; after a while they simply fell over the edge. I expect the last row of houses will be gone in another thirty years, and Sheepstone will be quite forgotten."

"It must be a weird place to live," I said, "with your garden getting smaller and the cliff-edge getting closer all the time. And what about the railway line? Is it safe?"

Grandmother laughed. "Quite safe, at least for a year or two, I should think."

Soon we were arriving in the town of Barcliff. It was smaller than Westhaven, but more expensive-looking. There was a golf club, a few good hotels, and a famous concert hall. Large houses stood proudly in well-kept gardens. One of them was no longer a house but a school – my new school.

You could tell that it had started life as a Victorian house, with turrets and wrought-iron balconies. On a dark night, it would have made a good setting for a horror film – from the front, that is. At the back and sides were modern bits like the Science block, the sports hall and tennis courts.

Grandmother looked round, taking it all in. (Perhaps this was the real reason why she had offered to come with me – to have a nose about.) She looked approvingly at the neatly-dressed girls walking up the drive. Some carried music cases, some had hockey sticks. All were quiet and well-behaved, possibly because a teacher was standing by the entrance, looking stern.

I had seen the outside of Neddy's school – his term had started two days earlier. It was nothing like this. The uniform, if people bothered to wear it, was scruffy; the pupils were a rowdy lot; the buildings had not been painted for years, except by spray-can. I was really glad my parents had chosen Barcliff.

"Grandmother," I said, "why did you think I ought to go to Edward's school instead of coming here?"

She looked startled. "Who told you that?"

"Mum."

"Well… it did occur to me that it might be easier for you to make friends in Westhaven. Barcliff is a good school, there's no doubt about it, but –" She didn't finish the sentence, because we were almost at the door.

What had she been about to say? Too late. I never found out.

My class had only fifteen people in it – all girls. I was not the only new arrival. The other one was a fat girl called Leila Green, who looked scared to death. Her hands trembled slightly; her face was damp and grey, like a used piece of chewing gum. I felt rather nervous myself, but at least I was better at hiding the fact.

The teacher asked two other girls to guide us around the school until we got to know it. My one, named Amy, didn't look too thrilled with this idea. She was a tall, fair, pretty girl, with a confident look about her.

At break, Amy showed me where the loos were, but when I came out I found that she'd vanished. Leila, the other new girl, had also been abandoned by her guide.

"Oh, help!" she wailed. "Where do we go now?"

"I haven't a clue," I said. "I'm new too, remember?"

She clutched my arm with plump, sweaty fingers. "Good. We can be friends then, can't we?"

I didn't answer. I already knew she wasn't the sort of person I wanted to have as a friend. I didn't even want to be seen with her, but she was hard to shake off. She followed me until at last we found our way outside, just as the bell rang for the end of break.

Amy did reappear then. She showed me the way to the next lesson, and afterwards took me to the dining-room. It was self-service, with quite a good choice of food, but while I was at the salad bar, Amy slid off again. She sat down at a table with a crowd of her friends, leaving me standing alone.

I saw Leila heading towards me with a huge plateful of chips. Pretending not to notice her, I followed Amy. Oh good – there was one spare place at the table.

"Mind if I join you?" I said, as casually as I could.

"Er... no. Of course not."

Nobody talked to me – but at least I didn't have to sit with Leila. She went off to a corner and started stuffing her face with chips. Comfort eating, I think they call it.

At last one of Amy's friends actually noticed I was there. She asked me where I lived.

"I've just moved to Westhaven."

"Oh... bad luck."

I almost said, "So what's wrong with Westhaven?" But that would have been a foolish move. Barcliff people, it was plain to see, looked down their noses at Westhaven.

"It *is* rather a dump," I said carelessly. "Luckily I'm only there for a year, while my parents are abroad. I actually live near Windsor."

Windsor, it seemed, was okay. After all, if it was good enough for the Queen...

Leila went back for seconds of chips, and Amy nudged her friend. "Look at that. Totally piggish."

"She'll blow up like a balloon," said one of the other girls.

"We ought to call her Lilo, not Leila," I said, and everyone laughed.

So that was how Leila Green became Green Lilo. I don't think she guessed it was my idea, because she kept on making pathetic efforts to be friendly for several days. Eventually I managed to freeze her out.

By that time I was in with the in-crowd. I was one of Amy's friends, a select little group: Caroline, Jessica, Lucy and me. We were probably the best-looking girls in the class, and certainly the liveliest.

Hard to make friends? Nonsense – it was easy. Grandmother need not have worried.

Chapter 4

Arguments

The one bad thing about my new school was the amount of homework. I had twice as much as Neddy; also, I got home later than he did because of the train journey. Quite often he was finishing his homework before I'd even started mine.

Grandmother, as you might expect, was strict about homework. No TV until the very last piece of work had been finished – so I often missed my favourite programmes. I couldn't even video them; Grandmother didn't have a video.

Meanwhile, Neddy would be out at a friend's house, or off bird-watching. Strangely enough, Grandmother didn't seem to mind when he went off on his own for hours and hours. (Mum would never have let *me* do that.)

Grandmother was strict about some things and quite relaxed about others. She liked people to be clean and tidy. But she never told Neddy off about the dreadful smells that sometimes came from his laboratory, right opposite my door. When I complained, she said, "I'm not going to stop him doing experiments. He's learned a lot from it. He always gets excellent marks in Science."

"It's all right for you, Grandmother," I said. "You don't sleep next to his smelly old lab. It wouldn't bother me nearly so much if I could have the guest bedroom."

Grandmother ignored this heavy hint. "You could always try opening your window," she said.

I found a way to get my own back on Neddy. When there was a TV programme he really wanted to watch – some boring old documentary about Space – I chose that moment to start my music practice. The piano was in the living-room, quite close to the TV.

"Alexa! Do you *have* to practise right now?" he asked.

"Of course I have to practise. I've got an exam coming up."

He turned the sound up louder. I played a piece called *Sweet Lullaby* at top volume and twice the normal speed.

He moved his chair closer to the TV. I pounded away at my scales and exercises, keeping my foot on the loud pedal. It sounded horrendous.

At last, in despair, Neddy switched the TV off. I stopped playing at once.

"Okay, I'll leave my practice till later," I said. "But you have to promise me something. No more bad smells."

"What on earth are you talking about? I did have a bath this morning."

"You know what I mean. No more chemistry experiments."

At that very moment, Grandmother came in. Surely she hadn't been listening at the door?

"Alexa," she said, "I would like a word with you."

Obediently I followed her into the kitchen. Once we were there, she didn't seem to know quite what to say – which was unusual for her.

"Were you and Edward arguing just now?" she asked.

"Well, not exactly arguing –"

She hesitated. "I realise this is not an easy time for you, Alexa. Having to move, to change schools and fit into a new household where the rules are different…"

I said nothing.

"But I do hope you and Edward are not going to make life impossible for each other. This is Edward's home too, you know."

"*He's* the one who's making life impossible," I said. "I just can't stand the smell of those chemicals. Yesterday the whole landing smelt of rotten eggs. It was disgusting."

Grandmother sighed. "I gave you a room near Edward's because I hoped the two of you would get on well together. But perhaps I was expecting too much. All right, Alexa. Have it your own way. You may move into the guest room, on condition that you live in peace with Edward, and move back upstairs whenever I have guests to stay."

"Oh, thank you, Grandmother!"

At once I started moving my belongings into the guest room. It was much nicer than the cramped little room on the floor above. There was a better view, more space to spread out my things, and a smell of lavender instead of rotten eggs.

While I was bringing another armful of clothes down, I met Neddy on the stairs. He gave me an odd sort of look.

"Tell me, Alexa," he said, "do you always get everything you want?"

"Usually," I said, smiling at him.

"There's a word for that, you know."

"Determined?"

"No. Spoilt."

And he vanished into his laboratory.

What he said made me angry. I was *not* spoilt! Neddy ought to see some of the girls I used to know. Marcella, for instance, who made a huge fuss until her parents bought her a pony, but then hardly ever went near it. Or Zoe, who had been on so many expensive holidays, there was nowhere left in the world that she wanted to visit. Or Carmel, who got twenty pounds a week just for pocket money.

Compared with them, I wasn't the least bit spoilt. But perhaps, compared to Neddy, I was. Neddy's life so far hadn't been too wonderful. Abandoned by his mother and father, brought up by Grandmother with her strict, old-fashioned ways… Perhaps that was the problem. Neddy was envious because I had parents who loved me, and gave me a few of the good things that money can buy.

Grandmother wasn't exactly mean, but she was careful with money. Neddy's bike was second-hand, his clothes were far from fashionable, and his trainers were positively medieval. Not that Neddy seemed to care – if you gave him a hundred pounds, he would probably spend it all on books or computer stuff.

"Does your dad send you any money?" I asked him once.

"Not any more. After he went to Melbourne, he

gradually stopped writing. I haven't heard from him in ages."

"You mean he doesn't even remember your birthday?"

Neddy shook his head.

"Perhaps he's got married again and had some more kids," I said. That was what Neddy's mother had done.

"I've no idea," said Neddy.

"Don't you mind about losing touch with him?"

"Look, are you stupid, or something?" he said very sharply. "Just try, for once, to imagine how somebody else feels. Think how *you* would feel if your parents never came back from the Far East – if they simply left you here."

"But they're not going to do that," I said, panicking slightly at the thought. "They are coming back."

"That's what my father told *me*. And I believed him."

I was angry now. Why was he trying to scare me? Of course Dad and Mum would come back, and anyway I would see them at Christmas. My flight was already booked.

"My parents would never abandon me like that," I said. "They're not the same as yours. They actually care about me."

Neddy's face flushed. "And my mother cares about me."

"In that case, why did she leave you with Grandmother?"

"It was because of the twins. They were born too early – they were in and out of hospital for months. She couldn't look after them and me, so I came to live here."

The twins were Neddy's sisters, or rather half-sisters. I had met them a couple of times – they were real terrors. At a family wedding, Charmain poured a whole jug of fruit juice all over the floor, and Verity took off her shoes so she could paddle in it.

"But the twins must be four or five years old by now," I said. "So why can't you go and live with your mum?"

"She sometimes asks me if I want to. I always say no. I hate it where she lives, and the twins are a pain, and I don't get on too well with their father. It's much more peaceful here at Grandmother's… or at least it used to be."

Before I arrived, is what he meant.

"So you actually like it here?" I said. "You sad person. I can't imagine anyone choosing to live here. Westhaven is such a hole – Grandmother should sell this house and move to somewhere nicer."

"Like Barcliff?" Neddy suggested.

"Yes, why not?"

"Because Barcliff is full of snobs with more money than sense. Oh yes, I can see why you like it so much."

"Shut up and leave me alone," I said. "Why don't you go to that lab of yours, and set off an explosion, and blow yourself to bits?"

Chapter 5

Losing

Although I had friends at Barcliff, in Westhaven I was
quite lonely. Two or three younger girls lived nearby,
but I thought they looked rather babyish. There were
no girls of my own age. A few boys sometimes hung
around in the Square. But they were Neddy's friends –
I didn't want to know them.

At weekends I was often bored. Grandmother suggested inviting my school friends to tea, but I didn't.
My Barcliff friends would think that Grandmother's
house was odd and Grandmother and Neddy were
quite peculiar. Afterwards they would laugh among
themselves, and pretend to feel sorry for me.

I also had the feeling that Grandmother would not
be too impressed with Amy, Caroline, Jessica or Lucy.
She wouldn't like their clothes or their manners. She
would disapprove of their endless talk about boys.

Amy had an actual boyfriend. He was away at
school, so she only saw him in the holidays, but she
talked about him all the time. Caroline and Lucy were
both in love with Jessica's older brother, who didn't
seem to take much notice of them. (Which was a good
thing. If he did ask one of them out, the other one

would hate her for ever.)

"Have *you* got a boyfriend, Alexa?" asked Lucy.

"No," I admitted. "There is this boy I rather like, though…" And I told them about Darren, the boy who lived at the corner of the street. I made him out to be older and better-looking than he really was. Of course I didn't mention the fact that he lived above a café, and would probably smell of chips, if I ever got close enough to find out. (I had seen him a few times, but never spoken to him.)

That was another reason not to invite my Barcliff friends to Westhaven. Yes – it was best to keep the two halves of my life completely separate.

One Friday night, when I was at a loose end, Grandmother said, "I don't like to see you looking so bored, Alexa. Why don't you go along to the Friday club with Edward?"

Neddy didn't look at all keen on this. Just to annoy him, I pretended to be interested. "What is the Friday club, exactly?"

"It's round at the church," he said reluctantly. "We do things like football or snooker or darts. Sometimes we watch a video."

"Sounds like a really wild evening," I said.

Grandmother said, "At least it would get you out of the house."

"But I wouldn't know anyone," I objected.

"You know Edward. And quite a few of the local children go. That nice boy Ben, and the Smith girls, and Darren Wheeler…"

It was the mention of Darren that decided it for me. Plus the fact that I was bored out of my brain.

"Okay, I'll try it," I said.

Grandmother was pleased – Neddy wasn't. Excellent!

We called for Neddy's friend Ben, who lived further along the Square. He looked surprised to see me, but – unlike Neddy – at least he talked to me on the way to the club.

It was in a church hall. I suppose there were about thirty kids there, girls as well as boys. A quick glance around showed me that Darren wasn't there. But it would look silly to turn round and go home straight away.

Two table-tennis tables had been set up; there seemed to be some kind of competition going on. "Come on! It's not too late to join in!" urged the man in charge.

I'm good at table-tennis – actually I'm good at most ball games. So I added my name to his list. It was to be a doubles contest. I was given a partner, a girl called Kay. She seemed quite friendly; we sat and chatted, waiting for our turn to play.

"Are you any good?" she asked me. "I'm not. I've only played it a few times."

My heart sank. I absolutely hate losing – it makes you look such an idiot.

"Why did you go in for the competition, then?" I asked.

"Oh, it'll be a laugh."

Yeah – a laugh for anyone who happened to be watching. Luckily Ben and Neddy had gone outside to play football.

Kay was right; she wasn't much good. But our opponents were even worse. We won that round quite easily. The next game was tougher – I had a fight on my hands. In the end, though, we won that too, or should I say I won?

"Wow, you're really good," said Kay. "You don't need me at all. You could play this on your own and still win."

"Not really," I said, trying to look modest. "You did a couple of great serves just now."

"We're in the semi-final now, do you realise?"

"Yes, I know." I would never have entered the contest if I hadn't believed I could get as far as this. As I said, I'm quite good, and I like to win.

In the semi-final we were up against two boys who looked a lot older than us. To begin with, they absolutely slaughtered us. We were losing 8-2, but then I began to get into the rhythm of the game. Kay had the sense to keep out of the firing-line.

I fought my way back. 11-4, 13-7, 15-10, 17-13… By now, quite a few people were watching and cheering us on. It felt like being on the Centre Court at Wimbledon.

The score was 18-17. "We can still do it," I whispered to Kay as she got ready to serve. But I could tell she was nervous. Her serve simply fell to pieces, and we lost.

Bitterly disappointed, I walked away, thinking that if I'd had a decent partner we could easily have won. It wasn't fair!

"Hey, wait!" someone called, grabbing my arm. I turned, and saw that it was Darren. I hadn't noticed him arriving; all my attention had been on the game.

He said, "What did you go and do that for?"

"Do what, exactly?"

"Lose like that. I really thought you could win it. I put money on you."

I said, "That was a bad move. How much did you bet?"

"Couple of quid. I'm totally skint now, and it's all your fault."

"Not *my* fault," I said indignantly. "My partner was useless."

"It is your fault. You were so good, you made it look like you couldn't lose. So now I reckon you owe me a drink."

What a nerve! I just stared at him. He grinned.

"Go on," he said, "you can afford it, can't you? Neddy says you've got pots of money."

I almost told him to get lost. But he *was* good-looking, and when he smiled like that...

"Okay then." There was a sort of shop in one corner of the hall, selling crisps and canned drinks. "What would you like? How about some mineral water?" I said, looking at him sideways.

"No, I hate that stuff. To me it tastes exactly like tap water," and he gave me that grin again. "I'll have a Coke. Cheers."

We watched part of the table-tennis final. It was between the boys who beat me and two girls half their size. The boys won so easily, it was boring.

"I reckon you would have wiped the floor with those girls," said Darren. "You deserved to win the whole thing."

Somehow I had stopped caring about losing. My mind was on what the girls at school would say, when I told them the latest on Darren. "I met him in this club on Friday night..." (I wouldn't say what kind of club it was. Let them think it was a night club.) "And we had a drink, and talked for ages. He's so nice. He looks just like Steve out of Seventh Heaven."

It was true, he did look like the lead singer in my favourite group. (He didn't sound like him, though. He had a Westhaven accent, which wouldn't impress Amy and the others. But then they were never going to meet him.)

Oh, if only he would ask me out! That really would be something to tell the girls about… But there wasn't time. People were folding up the tennis tables and putting chairs out in a circle.

"Oh-oh, here comes the boring bit," said Darren. "I'm off. See you around, Alexa."

Chapter 6

Stormy weather

What Darren called the boring bit was a short talk by Andy, the guy in charge. It was about church stuff – what Christians ought to be like. Darren was right, it wasn't exactly fascinating. But one thing I heard set me thinking.

Walking home with Ben and Neddy, I said, "Your church must be different from mine."

"I didn't know you went to church," said Neddy.

"I don't – well, not very often. Mum likes to go at Christmas and Easter, and she had me christened when I was a baby. But I've never heard anyone talk about 'becoming a Christian'. You just *are* one, aren't you? I mean, if you're English."

"Being English doesn't mean you're a Christian," said Ben. "You could be Jewish, or Moslem, or Hindu…"

"Or agnostic or atheist," said Neddy. (Typical. He loves using long words that no one else understands.)

"You what?" said Ben.

Neddy said, "Agnostic – you don't know if there is a God. Atheist – you're sure that there isn't."

"*I* don't know if there is a God," I said.

"In that case you're not a Christian," said Neddy. "You're an agnostic, like Grandmother."

"If God really exists," I said, "what does he look like? I've often wondered. Does he have a long grey beard and a white nightie? Doesn't he get bored sitting up there on a cloud all the time?"

"I told you she was childish," said Neddy to Ben.

Ben said, "But that's exactly how *you* used to talk, Neddy. Before…"

"Before what?" I asked.

"Before I knew there really is a God," said Neddy.

"Oh, you've 'become a Christian' then?" I said. "So why aren't you doing the things Andy said?"

"What things?"

"Weren't you even listening? Being nice to people. Acting all kind and helpful and good."

"I'm a lot more kind and helpful than *you* are," said Neddy angrily.

"Oh! Getting moody, are we? I'm sure Christians aren't meant to do that."

"You don't know the first thing about it," said Neddy. He began to walk faster, trying to leave Ben and me behind.

"Am I right, Ben?" I said loudly. "Aren't Christians supposed to be happy and joyful, not bad-tempered? That's what Andy was saying."

Ben looked uncomfortable. I could tell he didn't know what to say. He wanted to keep on the right side of both Neddy and me.

I said, "How can Neddy say *I'm* not a Christian, when he isn't one himself? He doesn't act like one."

Neddy must have heard this, but he didn't even turn his head. Ben said awkwardly, "I don't think… what I mean is, it's not up to us to judge who is or isn't a Christian. Only God knows that. Only God can see what goes on inside people's minds."

When he said this, I had a very odd feeling. I sort of pictured a trapdoor on top of my head. It was opening, and someone was shining a torch in, lighting up all the dust and cobwebs and bits of old rubbish that shouldn't be there…

Stop that! I slammed the trapdoor, shutting out the light. Was there really a God? And could he truly see inside people's minds? Probably not, I decided. That is… I hoped not.

A few days later I saw Darren again. I was on my way home from school, wearing my less-than-fashionable grey uniform. (However much you hitched up the skirt or loosened the tie, it still made you look about eight years old.) I rather hoped that Darren wouldn't notice me.

He was with a couple of boys I didn't know. They were lounging around outside the café, laughing about something. As I got closer the laughter stopped. I kept to the other side of the road; I didn't look at them. But I could feel them staring at me.

As I turned the corner into Fountain Square, I thought I heard one of them say something. "What a snobby little –" Had it been Darren who said it? I really didn't want him to think I was a snob. I wanted him to like me. And he *had* liked me, before he realised I went to Barcliff. If I saw him again I would talk to him, even if I was in uniform.

But the chance did not come. It was October now, and the evenings were dark and chilly. Westhaven was shutting down for the winter. All the sea-front stalls were closed and shuttered. The Corner Café was still open, but it didn't seem to be doing much business whenever I went past.

One Friday there was a terrific storm. I felt quite scared coming home on the train, especially when we crossed the viaduct. The tide was higher than I'd ever seen it. Huge waves were rolling in from the sea, breaking to white foam at the river-mouth. Wind-blown spray rattled against the windows of the train.

The woman opposite must have seen the anxious look on my face. "Don't worry, my love," she said. "This is nothing at all. Not compared with what happens in the winter-time."

I didn't find that thought particularly comforting. "You mean it gets worse than this?"

"A lot worse. Waves breaking right across the sea-front, that's what we had last year, and the Grand Hotel flooded out."

I asked Grandmother about it when I got home. "Do you often get storms here, Grandmother?"

"Not very often," she said. "Perhaps once a month in the winter. It's the price we pay for living by the sea."

I shivered. "I didn't know the seaside could be like this. I've only ever seen it in summer."

"*This* isn't much of a storm," said Neddy scornfully. "If you're frightened now, it's a good thing you weren't here last winter –"

"When there were waves breaking right across the sea-front," I interrupted. "And the Grand Hotel got flooded out – yeah, I know. Neddy, you're as bad as the old woman I met on the train."

Grandmother could see another argument building up. She said, "It was on nights like this that the wreckers used to go out, long ago. Have you heard about them, Alexa?"

I shook my head. Neddy sighed in a 'don't you know anything?' sort of way.

"In the days of sailing ships," said Grandmother, "a storm often meant that ships were blown onto the rocks and pounded by waves until they broke apart. Then the cargo would be washed ashore – casks of wine, or bales of cotton, or whatever the ship happened to be carrying."

"Along with the bodies of dead sailors," said Neddy.

Grandmother said, "The local people, who were poor fishermen, might get more from a good wreck than they could earn in a year. Some of them began to wish more ships would be wrecked – and they thought of a way to make it happen."

"How?"

"They went down to the shore on stormy nights, at places like Black Point, where rocks were hidden by shallow water. Then they showed lights that looked like the lights of the harbour mouth. If they were lucky, a storm-tossed ship, desperate to find a safe harbour, would sail straight onto the rocks."

"What nice people you have around here," I said.

"Oh, that was long ago," said Grandmother. "We're more civilised now, I hope."

"Anyway, there are proper lighthouses now," said Neddy. "And satellite navigation systems."

I said, "Do people really change? My dad always says there are some people who'd do anything for money…"

As I was soon to discover, my father was right.

Chapter 7

Finders keepers

By Saturday morning the storm had blown itself out. The air was quiet and peaceful. Seagulls were drifting over the town again, and diving with cries of joy onto the rubbish from spilt dustbins.

Feeling restless, I told Grandmother I was going out for a walk.

"Excellent idea," she said. "Would you like some sandwiches for a picnic lunch?"

"Not *that* long a walk," I said. I had been thinking of a gentle stroll down to the sea and back.

"It will do you good to get out of the house. You should make the most of the fine weather. Get some exercise. I wonder if Edward…?"

"No," I said. "I'd rather be on my own."

I walked along the sea-front. The tide was a long way out. In summer the beach would be crowded, bright with towels and sun umbrellas, noisy with children. Now the pale sands lay bare beneath a cold grey sky. A few lonely figures moved slowly across the vast emptiness. Two or three, I noticed, had metal detectors. They looked as if they were hoovering the sand. Did they ever find anything?

Just then, one of them began to dig in the sand. Curious to see what he found, I headed towards him. When he got up, I saw to my surprise that it was Darren.

"What have you found?" I asked. "Buried treasure?"

"Nah. Only an old rusty watch." He showed it to me, then flung it away along the beach. "I thought it would be good here today because of the storm, but it's rubbish. I've only found 50p."

"Why would the storm help?" I asked.

"It moves the sand around, see. Uncovers bits that used to be buried. Stirs everything up a bit."

"What are you looking for, exactly?"

He looked at me as if I was stupid. "Money, of course. Or anything valuable. I was down here every evening in the summertime."

"Really?" What a boring way to spend your time, I thought.

"Once," he said, "I found a purse with twenty quid in it, and I got loads of jewellery. Necklaces, rings and things. People are dead careless. They lie on the beach and money falls out of their pockets. They take their jewellery off when they sunbathe and lose it in the sand. Finders keepers, losers weepers!"

"You mean you keep the things you find? You don't hand them in to the police?"

"You're joking! No, I sell them. There's this shop in Down Street, they never ask no questions… and we need the money."

He picked up the machine again.

"Oh, can I have a go?" I said. "Please?"

He hesitated. "Okay, but if you find anything, it's mine."

"All right."

The metal detector was not much more than a stick with a flat ring on the end. Near the top was a dial like the speedometer of a car. I put the headphones on and swung the machine to and fro.

"Not too fast now," said Darren. "And keep it close to the ground, or you'll miss things."

I walked a few paces, listening carefully. Suddenly I heard a beeping noise.

"There's something there!" I said excitedly. "Look. Just here."

Darren began to dig. Very soon he uncovered a one-pound coin, and then another one. "Beginner's luck," he said. "Keep going."

But I found nothing else, apart from some foil wrapping and a cheap-looking bracelet.

"I reckon this beach is finished now until next summer," Darren said. "Trouble is, it's so easy to get to. There are too many people working it."

"Then why don't you try further along the coast?" I said. "From the train, it looks as if there are quite a few little bays between here and Barcliff."

"It's an idea," he said. "Thing is, they're not easy to get to, those places. You either have to go down the cliffs or right along the shore. Not many tourists ever get there."

"So? Not many metal detectors get there either, I bet. But anyway, I wasn't thinking of tourist rubbish. Small change and cheap jewellery – that's all you get from tourists. But what about the wreckers?"

Of course, being local, he had heard of the wreckers. "But that was ages ago," he objected. "What's going to be left after two hundred years?"

"I wouldn't know. Gold coins? Silver jewellery? That sort of thing doesn't rot or go rusty. If the wreckers didn't find all the stuff that got washed ashore, then maybe it's still there, hidden beneath the sand... just waiting to be found."

He stared at me. His eyes were alight with interest.

"Grandmother mentioned some place called Black Point," I said. "Where is it, do you know?"

"This side of Barcliff," he said. "But nothing could be buried there. Too rocky."

"Perhaps the wreckage didn't all come ashore just there, though. Perhaps some of it was washed along the coast, onto a sandy beach? It was stormy, remember – great big waves –"

"Dark, too," said Darren. "Yeah, I bet the wreckers did miss a few things. You're right, it's worth a look."

Then he said what I was hoping he'd say. Quite casually, as if he didn't care whether I said yes or no: "You want to come too?"

"Of course! Don't forget, it was my idea."

"And don't *you* forget, it's my metal detector. Anything we find, we split sixty-forty."

I nodded. "So how do we get there?"

"Across the river and along the shore. You better put some old trainers on. We might get wet feet."

"As a matter of fact, these *are* my old trainers. I've got three other pairs that are better than these."

He gave me a disbelieving look. His own shoes looked absolutely dreadful, and I remembered what he had said – "we need the money". Perhaps the Corner Café wasn't doing too well...

"Okay," he said, "you ready?"

For a minute I wondered if I should tell

Grandmother where I was going. But that would mean going back to Fountain Square... and she had, after all, told me to take a good long walk. Which was exactly what I was doing.

We crossed the river on a footbridge which was part of the railway viaduct. On the other side, a small path led along the shoreline. The tide was still quite low. We reached the mouth of the river and went on walking, out along the edge of the bay. At last we scrambled round a rocky point and found ourselves in another, much smaller bay.

Westhaven was out of sight by now. The little cove was deserted, apart from seagulls endlessly circling. The only sign of human existence was a narrow path which zigzagged up the cliffs.

"We could try this beach," I said. My legs were feeling tired.

"Nah, too easy to get to. You can bet someone's already been over it with a detector. We want some place that's not on a path. Some place that looks empty." He kicked an old Coke tin across the sand. "Some place nobody's been to for ages."

Round another point we went, and along a stretch of flat rocks, slippery with seaweed. "This will be underwater at high tide," said Darren. "We got to watch out for that, coming back."

I hardly heard him. I was imagining a pitch-black night, with great waves sweeping in, and a ship out there struggling towards harbour. A gleam of light on the shore – thankfully the sailors steered towards it. But they found no harbour, just wicked rocks that bit like teeth. And the sea swallowed them up...

Today it looked so calm, so harmless. Slow grey

waves rolled in, smooth as the backs of whales, and slid up the beach with a gentle hiss of foam. The rocks had given way to sand again. We had come to another small cove.

"This is more like it," said Darren. There was no path up the steep cliffs, no way in except the way we had come. "And that's a good sign, too." He pointed to the heaps of seaweed and driftwood at the foot of the cliff. I understood; if the sea washed things ashore here, it was probably doing the same thing two hundred years ago.

He started using the metal detector along the base of the cliff. Almost at once he got a signal, and I dug down eagerly. But all I found was a piece of rotting wood with a few nails in it.

"Oh great," I said, getting ready to chuck it away.

"Hold on. This could be a bit of a wrecked ship, couldn't it?"

"Looks more like a bit of somebody's garden shed."

Darren said, "Don't talk stupid. How would a garden shed get washed out to sea?"

"Stupid yourself. This could have come from Sheepstone – you know, the village that's falling down the cliff. A wrecked garden shed, lost at sea with its valuable cargo of lawnmower and spade and ancient bicycle."

Darren ignored me. With a frown of concentration, he was searching the beach again. After half an hour he had found a couple of rusty tin cans, lots more nails, and two worn bits of metal that could have been old pennies. I was getting bored with the whole thing – hungry, too. It was well past lunch time.

"This place is useless," I said. "Let's try somewhere else."

He shook his head obstinately. "Not yet."

I decided to play a trick on him. While his back was turned, I took off the gold necklace I was wearing. (It was rather nice – a gold chain with a dragon pendant whose eye was a tiny ruby. My parents had sent it from Singapore.) While Darren was busy digging, I quietly dropped it and pressed it into the sand with my foot. Then, taking careful note of the exact spot, I strolled away.

By now I was feeling quite angry with Darren. I'd been day-dreaming about him for weeks, but he didn't match up to the dream. He was good-looking – that was true. But it wasn't enough.

I didn't like his scruffy clothes or his meanness with money. I didn't like the way he ignored what I said half the time, as if I wasn't important. I didn't like him calling me stupid. What a nerve! He was the stupid one.

Casually I wandered by the edge of the sea, waiting to hear his excited yell when he found my necklace. But it didn't happen. I went back, and saw that he'd gone past the spot where I hid it. He must have missed it, the idiot.

Then I saw that the sand had been dug over in the place where I put the golden dragon.

"Oh, have you found anything?" I asked innocently.

"Yeah. More nails," he said. "Got enough to build a rowing-boat now, I reckon."

"Liar. What about the necklace?"

"What necklace?"

"*My* necklace," I said angrily. "You pig! You found it but you weren't even going to tell me! You'd have sold it and kept all the money!"

He grinned at me. "I found *a* necklace, yes. Nothing to say it's yours, though. I mean, it hasn't got your name on, has it?" He held it up and examined it.

"You said we would share the things we found! Anyway, it's mine. Give it back!"

I tried to snatch it, but he held it above my head, teasing me. I kicked him. He only laughed.

"What a nasty temper this girl's got," he said. "Warned you, didn't I? Finders keepers, losers weepers."

With a huge effort, I controlled my temper. He was bigger and stronger than me; I would never get the dragon back by force. I would have to persuade him.

"But I didn't lose it," I said. "I hid it on purpose. I wanted to give you a surprise."

"Wanted to fool me, more like. Wanted to get me all excited, and then say 'Give it back, it's mine.' Well tough. It's mine now."

"I'll tell Grandmother!"

This only made him smile.

"I'll tell the police! I'll tell them about the purse you found with twenty pounds in it. And about the shop that buys the things you dig up. I'm sure the police will be *very* interested in that."

"No, don't," he said hastily. "Tell you what, I'll sell it back to you."

"I'm not paying you for my own property!"

"Sixty-forty, we said, didn't we? Now if I sold this at the shop, they'd give me at least a tenner for it. Six quid for me, four for you. So pay me six quid and you can have it."

"All right," I said at once. I knew the gold dragon was worth much more than that.

"On one condition," he said. "Come out on a date with me."

What? You're joking, I wanted to say. I wouldn't go out with you if you were the last guy on earth!

But I wanted the jewel back. Dad would be upset if he knew I'd lost it.

"Well?" said Darren. "Yes or no?" He held the necklace just out of my reach.

"Yes," I said grudgingly. "Can I have it back now? Please?"

"Not yet." He put it away carefully in a zipped pocket. "When you've paid for it."

I stamped my foot in frustration. But you can't stamp very hard on sand.

"Hey!" Suddenly Darren looked alarmed. "See that tide. We better get going, or we won't make it round the point."

Behind our backs the tide had been creeping in. The little beach had shrunk to half its size. The rocks we had walked over were now under water – we would have to paddle. And the waves looked cold and grey.

"Come on!" said Darren. "Keep your shoes on. Get moving!"

The water was so cold, I almost screamed. I had rolled up my jeans to the knee, but soon the sea was deeper than that. Darren, ahead of me, was balancing the metal detector on his shoulder like a spear. A big wave came in, soaking him up to the waist.

And we weren't even close to the rocky point. How deep would it be out there? Over our heads?

"Darren," I said, trembling with cold and fear. "I can't swim."

"I can, but I don't want to. Not carrying this thing –

the water will ruin it. We better go back."

I didn't need telling twice. I splashed back through the shallow water and onto the beach. The dry patch of sand was now hardly bigger than a tennis court. On three sides the cliff walled it in. On the fourth was the tide, creeping closer and closer.

Just like the shipwrecked sailors of long ago, we were trapped.

Chapter 8

Rock-climbing

I tried to keep my voice steady. "How deep will it get at high tide?"

"That deep." Darren held his hand half a metre above my head.

"H-how do you know?"

He pointed to a line along the face of the cliff, where the rock seemed to change colour. "That's the high tide mark. We got to get above that." He didn't sound at all scared. He was carefully putting the metal detector away in his back-pack so that he would have both hands free for the climb.

I stared up at the cliff. Higher up, it looked as if you could climb it all right. It was steep, but not vertical like Beachy Head. There were grassy places between the outcrops of rock.

But down at the foot, where the sea washed against it, there was only rock, almost as steep as the wall of a house. A few cracks might give us small handholds and footholds... Darren was looking carefully for the best place to climb.

"Here, hold that." He gave me his back-pack. "And don't get it wet or I'll kill you."

He started to climb. At first he went up easily, but then, when his feet were higher than my head, the handholds stopped. He had to come back down to the beach.

But by now there was no beach. As the waves slid in, they came right to the foot of the cliff, soaking the sand, splashing my legs.

Darren waded knee-deep to reach another part of the cliff. This was better. He climbed swiftly; soon he was four or five metres above the water.

"There's a sort of a ledge up here," he called. "Should be safe enough. Think you can make it?"

I had only tried rock-climbing once. I wasn't bad at it, but that had been on the end of a rope, on a nice safe climbing wall, with an instructor to help.

"I don't know."

He was climbing down again. At first I thought it was purely to help me, but then I remembered his precious back-pack. When he had put it on, he said, "Okay. You go first."

He showed me the place to start. It looked utterly impossible. Then another wave came in, clutching like a hand around my knees. Which would be worse, to die quickly in a fall, or to drown slowly as the tide reached my neck… my chin… my mouth?

Stepping up on the first foothold, I gripped the rock with fingers that shook. My wet trainers felt slippery. When I looked up, the cliff seemed to lean out above me.

"I can't do this," I whispered.

"Yes you can," Darren said. "Go for it! Good hold to your left, up a bit. Now move your foot. No, the other one."

Slowly, very slowly, I inched my way up. Suddenly my foot slid off into space – I screamed, gripping on with all ten fingers.

"Don't panic. You're doing great, you're more than half-way. Right foot up a bit – there." His voice came from farther and farther below me, but I didn't dare look down.

At last, at last I hauled myself onto the ledge, and lay there, almost crying with relief. Swiftly Darren followed me up. He was a good climber, I had to admit. And extremely brave.

"Well, we made it." He grinned at me.

"Yeah. But what do we do now? Wait for the tide to go out again?"

"Could do."

"How long will that take?"

He looked at his watch. "High tide at around four. Then another two-three hours before we could get round the point again…"

"But it'll be dark by then! We can't go climbing about on rocks in the dark! And Grandmother will be having a fit."

"I told you, don't panic. We don't *have* to wait for the tide. We could go on up the cliff." Seeing the look on my face, he said, "You did the worst bit already. Look – the rest of it's easy."

I looked up. Compared with the rocks below us, it did look… not easy, no, but possible. It would be awfully high at the top though. What if my foot slipped again, right at the top?

"No. I don't want to."

"So what you going to do then?"

I said, "Shout for help, I suppose."

He laughed. "Who to – the seagulls?"

There was no one in sight. On the horizon was a long, low ship, so far away that it did not seem to move. Westhaven was only a couple of miles off, but it was out of sight around the angle of the cliff. This place was as lonely as the North Pole.

We could sit and wait to be rescued – but nobody knew where we were. Grandmother thought I had gone to the beach at Westhaven. It might be hours or even days before people searched for us as far afield as this. And we were wet and cold, getting colder every minute as our damp clothes dried on us.

"Perhaps you're right," I said.

So we began to climb.

As much as we could, we avoided the rocks. The grassy slopes between them were easier to climb. They were very steep – steeper than a playground slide, and just as slippery. Several times I lost my footing and slid backwards, clutching frantically at tufts of grass which came away in my hands. My knees were bruised. My hand was bleeding. I felt as if we'd been climbing for days, yet the cliff-top was still high above us.

"Stop!" I gasped. "I need a rest."

We sat down, leaning against a wall of rock. Cautiously I looked down. Far below us, seabirds flew over waves that looked no bigger than wrinkles in a table-cloth.

"Are we half-way up yet, do you think?"

"Could be." But once again he wasn't really listening to me. Something had caught his eye. He scrambled over a pile of loose rocks.

"Hey, look at this! It's a cave!"

"Oh great. A cave." I was too cold and weary to be interested in caves.

He pushed aside some of the rocks that half-hid the entrance. Then, on hands and knees, he crawled inside. I felt scared. What if he got lost in there? What on earth would I do then?

But he soon came out again. "Nothing there," he said.

"What did you expect to find? Pirate gold? The secret hoard of the wreckers?"

"Dunno. It would make a good hideout, though. You can't see it from up top or down below. You could live here, and no one would ever know."

Much later, I remembered that. But at the time it didn't seem important. I was tired and hungry and I wanted to go home.

Another long, stiff climb. All my bones seemed to ache by now, and my head swam with dizziness. But then, at last, I saw something wonderful outlined against the sky. A barbed-wire fence! A railway signal!

We climbed the fence and followed the long, downhill curve of the railway line. By the time Westhaven came into sight, dusk was falling. By the time we got to Fountain Square, it was quite dark, and I was so weary I could hardly put one foot in front of the other.

Grandmother was looking anxiously out of the window. Darren took one look at her face, and disappeared into the night without saying goodbye.

"Alexa!" Her voice was sharp. "Where on earth have you been? I expected you back hours ago. I was on the point of ringing the police. And who was that boy?"

Then she realised the state I was in. If she had been Mum, she would have hugged me and cried, but Grandmother wasn't a huggy sort of person.

She took my arm and led me indoors, helped me take my shoes off, and examined my sore, blistered feet. "First things first. You need some supper and a nice hot bath. And after that," she said ominously, "I want to know exactly what you've been up to."

Chapter 9

Win at all costs

"She was really mad at me," I told the girls at school. "And now she says I must always be home before dark, and always tell her where I'm going, and never go out with Darren again. It's not fair! Neddy doesn't have to keep all those stupid rules!"

"That's different," Grandmother had said when I complained. "You're a girl."

"I thought you were going to treat us both equally?"

She said coldly, "If you can prove to me that you're as sensible as Edward is, then I may allow you a little more freedom. But really, Alexa! Wandering off with Darren Wheeler – a boy you hardly know – going off into the wilds, and almost getting yourself drowned… whatever will your parents say?"

"Oh… Do you *have* to tell them?"

"Of course I must tell them. But I shall promise them that you won't be seeing any more of that boy. So keep away from him, Alexa."

"But *Grandmother*!"

If I wasn't allowed to see Darren, how could I get back my gold dragon? Besides, I wanted to see him again. It was easy to forget how mean he'd been over the necklace (naturally I didn't mention that to any-one), and remember only the good things about him. He was brave, he had saved me from danger, and best of all, he wanted to go out with me.

My friends all agreed that Grandmother was far too strict. After all, I was twelve now. Lots of twelve-year-olds went out with boys.

"You could always tell her you're visiting a friend," said Amy, "and then go out with Darren. She'd never know."

Caroline giggled. "I could ring you up and invite you over to my place, if you like."

"Maybe," I said cautiously. "But Grandmother would absolutely kill me if she found out. I would be grounded for years."

"How could she possibly find out?" said Amy.

"Go on, Alex," said Lucy. "*I* would. I wish I had a boyfriend."

"But who would go out with you, spotty-face?" said Caroline spitefully. An argument began. They were both still keen on Jessica's brother, who hardly knew they existed.

It was lunch hour; we were out in the school grounds. From one of the music practice rooms came the sound of a piano. It was playing a Chopin waltz, one of Mum's favourites – she often listened to it in the car. The sound of it filled me with longing… to see my parents, to go home again…

I listened. Whoever was playing, they were really good – probably someone in the Sixth Form. I glanced through the window and got the shock of my life, because the pianist was Leila Green. Fat old Lilo! I never guessed she could play like that.

When I showed the others, they were equally amazed.

"She's not really playing," said Amy. "She's miming to a CD."

"No she isn't. It's nearly as good as a CD, though."

Lucy said, "I hope she's not going in for the music contest."

The school music contest was only two days away. Lucy and I were planning to do a duet, flute and piano. We believed we had quite a good chance in the Under-14 section – but that was before we heard Lilo.

"I don't want to go in for it any more," I said.

"Why not?" said Lucy. "We might still come second."

"What's the good of that? Coming second to Lilo?" I always hated losing, but losing to Lilo would be three times as bad.

"Oh, go on," said Lucy. "Please, Alexa. I can't do it on my own."

Amy said, "Don't worry. We'll think of a way to sabotage Lilo."

"Slam the piano lid down on her fingers," suggested Caroline.

"Or put a drawing-pin on the stool," said Jessica, "and puncture her fat backside when she sits down."

Lucy made a noise like a balloon going down, and everyone laughed.

On the day of the competition, we were allowed to practise at lunchtime on the grand piano in the Hall. Lucy and I waited gloomily as Lilo practised her piece. It looked horribly difficult, full of sharps and flats, but she played it beautifully. No doubt about it – she would win.

When she had finished, she hurried off to lunch, leaving her music book on the piano. Lucy picked it up.

"Careless of her, leaving her music lying around," she said. "Suppose it just happened to go missing?"

"If it did, she would play something else," I said. "Like that Chopin thing she was practising the other day. And she'd still win."

"I don't mean the whole book. Just a page or two. Imagine – she starts playing, she sounds really good... the judges are impressed. Then she turns the page and oh dear, the rest of the piece isn't there! Confusion. Sudden stop. Lilo looks stupid again."

I said nothing.

Lucy took a page out of the loose-leaf music book. Looking around to make sure we were alone, she slid it behind a curtain at the back of the stage. She smiled. "There! If people can't take care of their things, what else do they expect?"

One bit of me was shocked. Another bit – the bit that wanted to win at all costs – made me smile and say, "Good idea." After all, winning was what mattered. Winners cheating, losers weeping...

The contest was scary. I had never played for such a big audience – the whole school, plus the Head and two music teachers.

Full of nerves, I started too fast, so that Lucy could hardly keep up with me. Both of us made mistakes. We didn't play nearly as well as we had during practice. People clapped politely as we sat down, pink with embarrassment.

But other people, equally nervous, made mistakes

too. I began to hope that we might be in with a chance, especially if Lilo ran into… a slight problem, shall we say.

It was her turn. She looked anxious as she went on stage, sat down and arranged her music. But when she started to play, it was as if there was no one else in the room. Her face was calm, her podgy fingers were swift and confident. She was playing brilliantly.

"Wow! She's as good as Miss Morley," Caroline whispered.

"Shhh."

The moment came – the page that wasn't there. I saw a flicker of surprise cross her face, but her hands did not falter. The music went on without a break. She knew it by heart, note-perfect.

When she finished, she got much more applause than anyone else. She deserved it, I thought grudgingly. She deserved to win. All the same, I hated her for it.

Lucy and I came fourth. I felt all chewed up inside, partly because of losing, partly because I felt guilty over what we'd done.

So when I passed Lilo in the corridor, I wasn't exactly nice to her.

"Congratulations," I said. "You played really well – for a fat girl."

Ha ha! That wiped the silly smile off her face.

Chapter 10

The Corner Café

I went to the Friday Club again, hoping that Darren would be there. But he didn't show up. What should I do? I could always go up to him in the street, if I saw him… but what if Grandmother found out?

At Boring Talk Time that evening we had a video instead of a talk. It was called *Winner/Loser*, so I gave it part of my attention. There was an interview with Jan Raven, who had had a million-selling CD a couple of years before. And several people groaned, because everyone knew what had happened to Jan. (Killed herself, all alone in a hotel room in Toronto.)

The interview had been filmed at the height of her fame. Her beautiful face glowed with pride and happiness. "Yes, I've got it all," she was saying. "Everything I ever wanted. Money and fame and someone who loves me." The word "WINNER?" flashed up on the screen.

Then there was a completely different scene – a refugee camp. A young doctor had given up her comfortable life in Britain, to work among sick and dying people. She had none of the good things in life. She was paid very little. Was she a LOSER?

Newspaper headlines told the shocking story which had raced around the world. "JAN RAVEN FOUND DEAD." "DOCTOR SAYS IT WAS SUICIDE." "DRINK AND DRUGS KILLED JAN."

And someone who knew her said, "She was quite a lonely person really. She couldn't handle all the fame, and then when her boyfriend left her, she just lost it completely…"

Of course you could guess what was coming next. The doctor in the refugee camp saying what a great time she was having, how wonderful it was to help people, blah blah blah. You were meant to think she was the winner and the world-famous pop star – the world-famous *dead* pop star – was the loser.

Andy switched off the video. He said, "It's like Jesus told people. *Whoever tries to gain his own life will lose it; but whoever loses his life for my sake will gain it.*"

I thought that was quite stupid. So winners were really losers, and losers were winners? What a load of rubbish.

Of course there was another way I could see Darren: I could go to the café. I didn't want to, partly because it would look as if I was chasing him. And partly because… well, quite frankly, the café was the sort of place I wouldn't normally be seen dead in. Even from the outside it looked cheap and grubby. The sign which said, 'Today's special – sausage, chips and beans', never changed from one week to the next. You could tell that the tablecloths would be plastic and the knives not very clean.

But I wanted to see Darren, almost as much as I

wanted my necklace back. When a week went by without a sign of him, I decided it was time to act. On Saturday, when Grandmother had gone out to the market, I got myself ready. I put on some make-up and my favourite earrings. Then, feeling rather nervous, I slipped round the corner of Fountain Square.

The café was almost empty. I sat down at a table away from the window (just in case Grandmother walked past). A tired-looking waitress, who was either very fat or expecting a baby, came to take my order. She looked a bit like Darren – his mother, perhaps?

"A Coke, please," I said.

I made it last as long as I could, although I felt rather odd sitting there alone. The only other customer paid up and went out. The room was quiet, apart from the slow whir of a fan, which could not freshen the hot, greasy air.

The place was so depressing. Tomato sauce was crusted around the necks of sauce bottles. There was a dead fly on the window-sill, and a sticky feeling on the floor beneath my feet. No wonder business was bad!

Still no sign of Darren. When the waitress slouched wearily past me, I said, "Excuse me."

"Yeah?"

"Er… is Darren around, by any chance?"

She stared at me, then nodded. "Upstairs."

"Could I talk to him, please?"

Again she gave me that unfriendly look. What was the matter? Was my voice too posh? Was my eye make-up smudged?

The woman went round behind the counter, opened a door and yelled upstairs. "Darren! Someone to see you."

"Who?" I heard him call.

"One of your lady friends."

One of them! How many did he have?

But when he appeared, I could tell by his smile that he was pleased to see me. And surprised.

"What are you doing here? Neddy told me your gran wasn't letting you out."

"Not exactly. I am allowed out, but I'm not supposed to see you. She thinks you're a bad influence."

"Well, I try," he said modestly. "What will she do to you if she finds out you're here? Give you a thousand lines?"

"She's not going to find out," I said. "Listen – I want my gold dragon back. You haven't sold it, have you?"

"Course not."

"Then where is it?"

"Here." He pulled down the neck of his T-shirt, and the gold dragon winked out at me.

"You're wearing it!" How romantic, I thought. Wearing it to remind him of me...

He said, "Yeah. Safest place for it. My kid sister wants to get her hands on it – nick anything, she would."

"I want it back," I said.

"Sure. But you know what I said – it'll cost you."

"Here's the money you asked for." I held out the six pounds. He took the money, kissed it, and put it in his pocket. His mother, I noticed, was watching us while pretending to wipe the counter.

"So when are you coming out with me?" he said. "How about tonight? We could go and see that new horror film –"

"I can't. Not tonight." I explained that I would have to pretend one of my school friends had invited me over.

"Next Friday any good?"

"All right. If I can fix it with Caroline."

He looked pleased. "Yes! Wait till I tell Macaulay!"

"Who's Macaulay?"

"Mate of mine. He said I'd never get you to go out with me. Barcliff girls are all snobs, he says. He'll be sick as a parrot."

I asked him where I should meet him.

"How about outside the Odeon, seven o'clock? We could see *House of Horror*."

"Isn't that a 15?"

"Who cares? They never check. Anyway you look fifteen all right, when you're dressed up."

I wasn't at all sure I wanted to see *House of Horror*. But if that was what it took to get my necklace back…

A silence fell. Darren's mother had gone out to the kitchen; I heard the clatter of plates.

"How's the metal detecting?" I asked, to fill the gap. "Have you found that chest of gold yet?"

"Nah," he said gloomily. "I've been out a couple of times and got nothing. Think I'll pack it in until next summer. There must be another way to get money!"

"There are lots of ways," I said. "A paper round, a Saturday job…"

Suddenly he was angry. "What do *you* know about it? You've never even tried to find a Saturday job, I bet. You're rolling in money."

"Well, I could lend you some," I said.

"Oh sure. You could lend me some. Know how much we need? Ten thousand pounds."

"What?" I gasped.

"Ten thousand pounds."

"Whatever for?"

"My dad got this loan off the bank. It was to get us through a bad patch – that summer when it never stopped raining. He thought he could pay them when we got a good summer. But he couldn't, and now the bank wants the money back."

"So what will happen?"

"They could make us sell up." He looked utterly miserable. "They could put us out on the street. No home, no work. And Mum's expecting, too."

I looked around at the dismal room. It wouldn't break *my* heart to leave the place, but Darren might feel differently. This was his home, after all. He had never known anywhere better.

"What would you do?" I asked.

"I dunno. Mum and Dad have rows about it all the time… I think Mum would walk out if it wasn't for the baby."

He stopped talking, because his mother had opened the kitchen door. She struggled out with a tray of cups. She looked as if she needed to sit down, put her feet up, and have someone bring her a nice cup of tea. Instead, she had to keep working. I understood now why she was so grumpy.

And Darren – I saw why he was so mean about money. I only wished there was something I could do. If it had been ten pounds, or a hundred, I could have helped him easily. But ten thousand!

"I'd better go," I said awkwardly. "Grandmother could come back anytime."

"Yeah. Bye then."

"See you on Friday." I would buy the cinema tickets, I decided. It was the least I could do.

Outside, the cold sea wind smelled wonderful. I stood on the pavement and breathed in deeply, clearing my lungs of smoke and grease. An old lady who was passing gave me a rather odd look.

Then I hurried back home. But it was all right – Grandmother was still out. My secret was safe.

Chapter 11

Phone messages

That night there was a phone call. Grandmother answered it. I heard her voice turn suddenly sharp.

"But Susan! We arranged it months ago. He's been looking forward to it." A pause, and then she said cold-ly, "I really don't see why I should. You must break the news to him yourself. Edward! Your mother has something to tell you."

When Neddy put the phone down, his face was quite expressionless.

"What's the matter?" I asked him.

"Nothing," he said, and went upstairs.

"Is anything wrong?" I said to Grandmother.

She said angrily, "Susan is being selfish again. She and Roger have decided to take their daughters to Disneyworld, which means that Edward won't be able to spend his half-term with them."

"Why don't they take him to Disneyworld, too?"

"Apparently they booked a cut-price package for a family of four. It would be too expensive to take Edward as well – that's Susan's excuse. The truth of the matter is, Edward and Roger don't get on, and Susan always puts Roger first."

Grandmother must be really angry, or she wouldn't be telling me all this. Roger, of course, was Neddy's step-father. Perhaps he was part of the reason for Neddy living at Grandmother's house instead of with his mother.

"Is Neddy – I mean Edward – upset?" I asked.

"I imagine he is. It's not the first time this sort of thing has happened. Try to be nice to him in the next few days, Alexa."

I might have done, but I hardly saw him. He spent most of the weekend in his laboratory. Instead of bad smells, loud noises came out of it – hammering and drilling noises. I could hear them even from the floor below.

"Why does he have to make such a terrible racket?" I complained to Grandmother.

"I'm sure he has his reasons," was all she would say.

"What on earth are you making in your lab?" I asked him when we were washing up. (Despite all my efforts and several breakages, I hadn't been able to get out of doing this.)

"Nothing you would understand," he said.

That annoyed me. "I suppose it's a time machine. Or a tactical nuclear missile."

He didn't answer, which annoyed me even more.

"It's such a pity you're not going to Disneyworld," I said. "You'd love Epcot – it's all about science. Didn't you *want* to go?"

"I didn't get the chance," he said.

"Oh!" I tried to sound surprised. "But if all your family are going, why don't they want you?"

"My family are a complete waste of space," he said bitterly. "I wouldn't care if I never saw any of them again. Including cousins." He shot me a look full of hatred.

"You're upset," I said in a soothing voice. "I don't blame you. All of them going to America and leaving you behind! Anyone would be upset."

Crash! The glass he was drying hit the floor. He didn't stop to sweep up the mess – he went out, slamming the door.

Another round to me.

On Monday, I told my friends about my date with Darren. They were impressed.

"Where's he taking you?"

"What are you going to wear?"

"Nothing special," I said casually. "We're only going to the cinema."

"*Only* going to the cinema…" Lucy sounded envious. "I wish I was only going to the cinema with a boy."

Even Amy looked as if she wouldn't mind swapping places with me. (Her own boyfriend hadn't written for weeks. We were starting to suspect that he'd dumped her.)

Caroline was eager to provide me with a cover story. "I'll get Mum to ring your grandmother, asking if you can come over on Friday."

"But what will your mother think when I don't turn up?" I said.

"I'll tell her you're ill."

It seemed quite safe, but somehow I felt uneasy. All those lies… well, not lies exactly. I *was* going out on Friday – though not with Caroline. Anyway, I wouldn't need to lie, if Grandmother wasn't so ridiculously strict.

When I got home from school I saw at once that I was in trouble. She had that Head Teacher look on her face again. (I bet no one used to talk during Assembly at her old school. That look would have frozen them solid.)

"Alexa," she said. "Come here."

Neddy, going upstairs, gave me a sort of gloating smile. I'm sure he wanted to hear me being told off, but Grandmother led me into the living-room and closed the door firmly.

"Is it true, Alexa, that you've been visiting the Corner Café?"

Her sharp grey eyes searched my face. I felt myself going red.

"I only went there once," I muttered.

"Why, might I ask?"

"I was thirsty and I felt like having a Coke. I'm tired of fruit juice." (Coke was one of the many things that Grandmother never bought. She disapproved of it, along with fast food and battery hens and red meat and anything that was advertised on TV.)

She said, "Don't lie to me! You went there to see that boy Darren. After I'd expressly forbidden you to see him again!"

Grandmother hated disobedience. She also hated lies. I decided it would be safer to tell the truth... or part of it.

"But I had to see him," I said. "He had something that belonged to me – my dragon necklace."

"Then why didn't you tell me? I could have got it back for you. Instead of which, you chose to be disobedient."

I was silent.

"What I am waiting for," she said frostily, "is an apology."

"Oh. I'm sorry, Grandmother."

"And a promise that you won't do it again."

That was easy. "I promise I'll never go to the café again."

Notice, I didn't promise not to see Darren again. Grandmother was clever – but not clever enough to pick up on that.

Rather awkwardly, she put a hand on my shoulder. "You know, Alexa, I'm doing this for your own good. That boy is quite unreliable. In any case you're far too young to be hanging around with boys. There will be plenty of time for that when you're older."

The phone rang. From what Grandmother said, I could guess she was talking to Caroline's mother.

"How nice! Yes, I'm sure Alexa would enjoy that… Well, that's very kind of you. I'm glad Alexa is starting to make some friends. It's never easy for a new girl…" She talked about me as if I wasn't there, or had suddenly gone deaf.

She put the phone down. "It's all arranged. You're going to your friend's house after school on Friday. Her mother is quite happy to have you there all evening, and bring you back in her car, as it's rather late to be travelling alone on the train. She sounded very nice."

I smiled. The "lift home" wouldn't be a problem. I would tell Grandmother, when I got in, that Caroline's mother had dropped me off at the corner. She would never know that it was actually Darren I had just said goodbye to. (Or even kissed goodbye?)

"How lovely," I said politely. "I'm really looking forward to Friday."

Chapter 12

Behind the curtain

One question was bothering me. Who had told Grandmother about my visit to the café? If she had seen me herself, she would have tackled me about it straight away. No – someone else must have seen me go in or leave, and then told her later.

I was quite sure that someone was Neddy. He was angry with me, so he'd decided to make trouble. Well, I wasn't going to let him get away with that. I started looking for some way of getting my own back.

The best idea – the thing that would really hurt him – would be to do some damage to his beloved laboratory. I had never actually been inside it, only caught a glimpse through the open door. It was a small room, crowded with equipment which looked expensive and breakable.

The problem would be getting in there. At the moment, Neddy seemed to spend his entire life in the lab. He only came out at mealtimes.

But then I remembered – he usually came home late from school on Tuesdays. It was Chess Club, or something equally boring. On Tuesday I hurried home from the station, hoping that for once, just for once,

Grandmother wouldn't make me do my homework straight away.

No chance. I zipped through my Maths and French at top speed; Grandmother was quite impressed.

"You see what you can do, Alexa, when you really buckle down to it? All it takes is a little concentration."

Neddy was still out. I slipped upstairs and quietly opened the door of the lab. Now that I saw it properly I thought it was a very odd room. It had rose-patterned wallpaper and long velvet curtains, left over from its previous life as a bedroom. It also had shelves and shelves of scientific apparatus and mysterious things in jars. A white lab coat hung behind the door. There was a faint, chemical smell from old experiments.

I could see now what all the hammering had been for. Neddy was making a long wooden table, like the lab benches at school. It was nearly finished; I wondered if I could sabotage it. Saw through the legs, perhaps, so that when it was loaded with equipment, the whole thing would crash to the floor?

Or how about mixing up the contents of those neatly labelled jars? Careful, now. Don't get carried away. We don't want the entire house to vanish in one mighty explosion.

Suddenly I heard feet on the stairs, and voices. Help! Neddy mustn't find me in here!

I rushed towards the window, thinking I could climb out onto the balcony. But a big telescope on a stand blocked my way. Then I saw that there was space to hide behind the thick floor-length curtains. As I squeezed into the gap and held my breath, I heard two people come in.

"Wow! Did you make this yourself?" It was Neddy's friend Ben, I guessed by the voice. "Amazing. It must have taken ages."

Neddy said, "Shut the door, please. I don't want *her* listening on the stairs."

Did he mean Grandmother? No, it was me he was talking about.

"I really can't stand that girl," he said in a low voice. "Everything was fine until she came to live here, but now... She's always getting at me, trying to put me down. She has to have her own way all the time and win every argument. I hate her!"

Ben said, "I know what you mean. It's like the only way she can feel good is by making other people feel bad."

"She reminds me of that kids' game, *I'm the king of the castle*. She spends her entire life playing that."

"Yeah," said Ben. "Trying to stay on top by pushing everyone else out of the way."

I was surprised and angry. It seemed as if Ben didn't like me any more than Neddy did. (Why? What had I ever done to him?)

"I think she's quite a sad person," Ben went on. "She won't have any friends if she carries on like this."

What rubbish! Of course I had friends, lots of friends. Amy, Caroline, Jessica and Lucy – they all liked me. So did Darren.

"And she thinks she's so clever," Neddy was saying, "but actually she's as thick as two short planks. Grandmother told her to keep away from Darren, so guess what she did – went to the café on Saturday, in broad daylight, right in front of Miss Grindlay!"

Neddy put on an old-woman voice. "I'm surprised

you allow your granddaughter to frequent that dreadful place. It breaks every hygiene law in the book, besides attracting quite the wrong sort of person to Fountain Square."

Ben laughed. "So what did your grandmother do? Ground Alexa for a month?"

"No," said Neddy gloomily. "Only shouted at her and made her promise not to do it again. It's so unfair! She wouldn't have let *me* off like that!"

"Perhaps she feels sorry for Alexa. A spoilt only child, who's always had everything she ever wanted, until suddenly her parents go off and leave her…"

"What about me?" said Neddy. "I'm an only child too – or as good as. And my parents went off and left me. But I don't behave like she does!"

I was starting to boil with fury. It was worse because I had to stay absolutely still, in case the curtain moved. I couldn't bear it if they found me now… I would look such an idiot.

Neddy said, "The worst thing is, I can think of lots of ways to put her in her place. I lie awake at night thinking about it. But I can never actually do it."

"Why not?"

"You know why not. Because I'm a Christian now. Love your enemies, do good to those who hate you, and all that."

Ben said, "But it's just as wrong thinking bad thoughts as actually doing them. That's what it says in the Bible."

"What?" Neddy sounded startled.

"Jesus said that feeling angry with someone is as bad as murdering them."

"But… that's not fair," said Neddy. "I can't *help*

feeling angry. It just happens, every time I think about her."

"My grandad told me something once," said Ben. "When I kept feeling mad at my sister, he said I should pray for her every time I felt angry. And you know something? It really worked."

"What do you mean, it worked? Your sister is still pretty awful."

"Yes, but *I* don't get so angry any more."

"Perhaps I'll try it," said Neddy rather doubtfully.

Behind the curtain, I clenched my fists. Yes, go on and try it, you stupid fool! It won't make any difference. I'm going to make you so angry you'll practically catch fire!

I stopped listening to what they said. My mind was spinning with thoughts of revenge for all the foul things they'd said about me.

Push Neddy's telescope over the balcony. Put his homework in the dustbin. Release his pet stick insects. Set the lab on fire –

No, stop. Control yourself. Behaviour like that would be dangerous and childish, and anyway it would get you into trouble. Think of something more subtle – more hurtful.

I began to have an idea...

Suddenly I heard Ben say, "Time I went," and the door opened. I held my breath. Would Neddy leave the room too, or would he stay? I couldn't stay hidden much longer; I could feel a sneeze coming on.

Luckily they both went out, and I heard two sets of feet on the stairs. Cautiously, very cautiously, I slipped out of my hiding place. There was just time to glide across the landing into the empty room which had once been mine. Then Neddy came back upstairs. Without seeing me, he went into the lab.

Feeling weak with relief, I wandered over to the window. This was where I had caught my first glimpse of Darren, down in the back yard of the café. Without much hope, I looked for him again – and there he was.

Another boy was with him. Was that Macaulay, the friend he had mentioned? He looked a bit older than Darren; he also looked tougher. His face was lean and narrow, like a fox.

Both boys were smoking. That was probably why they were skulking around in the rubbish-strewn yard. They weren't there for the scenery, that was certain.

I knocked on the window, and Darren looked up. He saw me, grinned and waved. Then he nudged his friend, who gave me a long, cool stare. Darren said something that I couldn't hear. The other boy looked disbelieving.

Aha! Darren must have told him we had a date on Friday. All at once I felt happier. Whatever Neddy thought about me, it didn't count, because of Darren. Darren was much better-looking than Neddy would ever be. Darren liked me. Darren had boasted about me to his friend.

As for Ben and Neddy – who cared about them? Stupid little boys. That's all they were.

Chapter 13

Safe enough

Next morning, when I left the house, I was surprised to see a police car parked two doors down. That house belonged to two elderly sisters. They were so ancient and pale and faded that I couldn't imagine them being in trouble with the police. Maybe one of them had died, or something.

In the afternoon the police car was gone, but there were two workmen doing something to a basement window. And at home, Grandmother and Neddy were outside, looking at our own basement window. They were down in the narrow space that Grandmother calls the "area", which is a kind of sunken yard between the house and the street.

I went down the steps to see what they were doing. I had never been down here before. There was a coal-hole under the pavement, a large dustbin and a smell of cats.

"That seems safe enough," Grandmother was saying to Neddy. "Oh, hello, Alexa. How was school today?"

"Not too bad. But what's going on? Has there been a break-in?"

"I'm afraid there has – at the James's house. They got in through a basement window during the night."

"Did much get taken?" I asked.

"All their jewellery. But luckily no one was hurt. The Jameses are both as deaf as a post; they slept through the whole thing."

"Was it worth a lot of money?"

"Several thousand pounds, or so Sheila Grindlay tells me. Of course it was insured. But I don't think the James sisters feel safe in their own home any more."

"They should have had a burglar alarm," I said.

Grandmother sighed. "I'm afraid, like me, they're old enough to remember a time when people were more honest. But I believe they're having an alarm put in now."

"We ought to get one too," said Neddy. "I could fit it."

"A decent alarm would be expensive," said Grandmother. "Anyway, I don't possess much that's worth stealing."

"There's my jewellery," I said.

Neddy said, "What about all my lab equipment? My telescope is worth quite a lot."

"Your telescope is probably safe enough," Grandmother reassured him. "Burglars usually take small items which are easy to sell. But your jewellery, Alexa... how much is it worth?"

"I don't really know. Some of it is quite good. Mum always tells me to look after my gold bracelets – they were her grandmother's. And my blue ring is a real sapphire."

"Those things would be safer under lock and key," said Grandmother. "Where are they now?"

"In my bedroom. In a drawer."

"That's right, tell the whole street," said Neddy.

Footsteps went rapidly by on the pavement above. Just for a second I felt uneasy. Could anyone really have heard what I said?

I decided I would find a safe hiding-place for my jewel case. Having Grandmother lock it away was not a good idea, because I wouldn't be able to wear my things whenever I wanted them.

"How did the house get broken into?" I asked.

"Like this."

The basement window was the old-fashioned sash type. There were two sections held shut by a metal catch. Over the years, the wooden frame had warped slightly, leaving a narrow gap. Neddy slid the blade of his penknife through and released the catch.

I tried to open the window, but it wouldn't budge. "That's because we've fitted modern safety catches as well," Grandmother explained. "They can only be undone from inside the room."

"We ought to do the same with the windows at the back of the house," said Neddy.

"Oh, I think the back is safe," said Grandmother. "After all, how could a burglar get round there? There's no access from the street."

She was right. The only way to reach the back windows was by going through the house, or else climbing over the wall from a neighbouring garden. The little row of gardens lay between Fountain Square and Pump Street, entirely enclosed by buildings.

All the same, as I lay in bed that night, I couldn't help worrying slightly. Suppose a burglar did get around to the back of the house? He could break into a neighbour's house from the front, go out at the back, climb over our garden wall... and then the knife would silently slide back the window catch, the window would open...

I listened fearfully, half-expecting to hear a loud crash as the intruder fell over in the basement. (There was so much junk stored down there – broken furniture, old deck-chairs, Grandmother's historic bicycle – that it was as good as a burglar alarm.)

But the house was silent, apart from the steady tick of the grandfather clock on the landing. I got out of bed and took my jewel case from its drawer. Where should I hide it? After trying and rejecting various places, I settled on the fireplace. I wrapped the box in a pillow-case to keep it clean, and slid it under the grate. The fireplace hadn't been used for years, because of the central heating, so it would be perfectly safe.

Grandmother suddenly announced that she was going up to London for the day. She wanted to do some shopping before the Christmas rush.

"Can't I go too?" I pleaded. I hadn't been on a shopping trip since Mum went away.

"No, you cannot. You'll be in school. Also, your Christmas present is one of the things I shall be buying."

Wonderful. Without me there to drop hints, what would she buy me? For my birthday she'd given me a pair of woolly gloves and a copy of *Pride and Prejudice*.

"I shall go on Friday. You'll be at your friend's house after school, Alexa, so I won't have to hurry back. Edward, I've arranged for you to eat at Ben's house on Friday."

This was excellent news. It would solve the last problem about Friday evening – where to get changed for my date with Darren, and how to fill in the time after school. If Grandmother had been at home, I would have had to hang around the shopping mall and get changed in the toilets. Now I could simply go home, and let myself in with my key.

What if Neddy saw me, though? He would be at Ben's house, but that was nearby. He might tell Grandmother I was at home when I was meant to be at Caroline's. I would have to invent some story about Caroline being ill... Oh, don't worry. It probably wouldn't happen.

"Everything's falling into place," I told the girls at school. "I can hardly wait for seven o'clock on Friday."

"Where are you meeting him?" asked Lucy.

"Outside the Odeon. We're going to see *House of Horror*. It's a 15, but of course Darren could easily pass for fifteen, he's so tall."

"He sounds too good to be true, this guy," said Jessica enviously.

Caroline said, "Whatever you do, Alexa, wear something that makes you look a bit older. Wouldn't it be sad if they let Darren into the cinema and not you?"

"Tragic," I said, "but it's all right, Darren says they never check."

"Darren, Darren, Darren," said Amy. "Know something? I'm getting sick of the sound of that name."

So we talked about something else. I didn't mind. I knew she only said it because she was jealous.

Neddy was back to his normal self. He had stopped hiding in the lab for hours on end; he seemed to have forgotten the Disneyworld trip. It was time to put my plan into action.

While I was doing my homework, he went out to a friend's house. When he came back I told him his mother had rung. "She wants you to call back after eight o'clock."

"Did she say what it was about?"

"I'm not sure – I couldn't hear too well, she was on a mobile. Something about Roger being ill, and a spare ticket…"

Neddy's face lit up. "Roger's ill and can't go to America? So I can go in his place?"

"Could be," I said casually. "But she said not to ring before eight because she would be at the hospital."

"Hospital… that sounds serious." He didn't seem too upset at the idea.

During the next three hours, I noticed how often he looked at the clock. The moment it struck eight, he rushed to the phone.

"It's me. Edward. Can I speak to Mum?" A look of surprise crossed his face. "Gone out? But she called earlier, asking me to ring her at eight… Is that Roger? Oh. I got some kind of garbled message earlier, that you were ill in hospital… Okay. Must be a mistake."

He glared at me across the room. I smiled back.

"Yes," he said, "I bet the twins are really excited… Oh, it doesn't matter. I didn't actually want to go. Have a nice time… Bye."

Grandmother looked up from her book. "What was that all about, Edward?"

Would he tell on me? But no, he said what I knew

he would say. "Oh nothing."

Then he went off upstairs. I wondered if he remembered Ben's useful advice about what to do if you hate someone. Probably not. More likely he was reading up on arsenic and strychnine, and imagining the effects if he put them in my coffee.

I chalked up another win.

Chapter 14

A night to remember

At last it was Friday. I sat on the afternoon train, trying to look calm, but finding it difficult. A huge smile kept spreading over my face.

I looked pityingly at the other girls on the train. None of them, I was certain, would be going out that night on their first real date. None of them had a boyfriend like Darren.

Arriving home, I opened the door cautiously and listened. It would be very awkward if Grandmother had changed her mind about the London trip… But the house was silent and empty. I could do exactly as I liked.

I made myself a sandwich, remembering to tidy up carefully afterwards, so that Grandmother wouldn't wonder who had been in the kitchen. Then I ran a nice deep bath and lay in it for ages. (Grandmother didn't approve of long, hot baths. When she was a girl, in the War, you couldn't have more than four inches of bathwater, she was always telling me.)

I dried my hair, trying to decide what to wear. It would be a mistake to look too smart; Darren would probably appear in the black leather jacket that he wore everywhere. On the other hand, I wanted to look older than I really was. In the end I settled for jeans and a tight black top. It needed some jewellery, so I wore a plain gold chain. When Darren gave me my dragon necklace, I was planning to give him the plain gold chain to keep. I wouldn't miss it – I had several of them.

I put on some eye make-up which I'd bought specially; then I changed it because I didn't like the colour. I was starting to feel a bit nervous. My first date… I really wanted it to go well. I wanted it to be an evening I'd never forget.

At last I was ready. It was a quarter to seven. I put all the lights out, so that Grandmother would find the house exactly as she'd left it. Then I went out, being careful to lock the door.

Outside, the night was dark and chilly. Westhaven was quite different from its summer self, when visitors wandered the streets throughout the long light evenings. Now most of the shops were shut; the fairground was silent. The town, like a tired animal, was quietly going to sleep for the winter. It might have been depressing, but nothing could dampen my mood that night.

I reached the cinema at two minutes to seven. Darren wasn't there, but that didn't surprise me. He wasn't the sort of person who would be good at turning up on time. Looking at the posters, I saw that *House of Horror* didn't start until half past seven, so there was no hurry.

Soon I began to feel cold – I should have worn a thicker jacket. Perhaps I should wait inside? No, he'd said "outside the Odeon". If I went in, we might miss each other.

People were arriving now in pairs and groups. I amused myself by trying to guess which film they were going to see. That romantic couple, arms entwined, were clearly heading for *Love Match*. The father with his excited kids was going to see *Space Wars*. The gang of teenage boys would be *House of Horror* fans.

Just then one of the boys detached himself from the group. As he came towards me, I recognised him – Darren's friend Macaulay.

"Are you Alexa?" he said.

I nodded.

"Pity. I bet Darren a fiver you wouldn't go out with him." He smiled at me – not a very nice smile.

"Where is Darren?" I said rather coldly.

"Oh, he said to tell you he'll be a bit late. His mum's ill and his dad made him help out at the café."

"Do you know how long he'll be?"

"Nope. Why don't you come out with me instead? I could give you a *much* better time." And he smiled that wolfish smile again.

"No thanks," I said.

He laughed. "Suit yourself," he said, and went back to his friends. He told them something which made them all stare at me; I was glad when they went into the cinema.

I started walking up and down to keep warm. After a while I looked at my watch – twenty past seven. Perhaps I ought to buy the tickets. Otherwise we might miss the start of the film.

Keeping one eye on the entrance, in case he turned up, I bought two tickets for *House of Horror*. Then I went back outside, shivering as the cold wind touched me again.

And something else touched me – a hand on my shoulder. I turned with a welcoming smile, which faded at once. It wasn't Darren who had crept up behind me, but Amy, Caroline, Jessica and Lucy.

"Well? Where is he?" demanded Amy. "Where's the famous Darren?"

I stared at her. "What are you doing here?"

"Going to the cinema, of course. We decided to slum it in Westhaven for a change. Any objection?"

"You've been spying on me!" I said angrily.

"Not *spying*," said Lucy. "But we did just happen to find a café over there…"

"With a perfect view of the Odeon." Caroline giggled. "You've talked so much about Darren, we couldn't bear not to see him for ourselves."

"But it looks as if we're going to be disappointed," said Amy. "It looks as if he's decided not to bother."

"What a shame," said Jessica.

"Tragic," agreed Lucy.

"I wonder why he's stood you up?" said Caroline. "Surely he can't be tired of you already."

"He hasn't stood me up!" I cried. "He's late, that's all. He sent his friend with a message."

Amy said, "So that was his friend, was it? The yobbo you were talking to earlier?"

"I don't think much of his taste in friends," Caroline said, grinning. "If Darren's anything like *him*, you can keep him."

Careful, now. Don't get mad – they'd enjoy it. Don't let them see how they're getting to you… But why are they being so nasty? They're supposed to be friends!

"I suppose this was all your idea," I said to Amy, and she smirked at me. "Just because your boyfriend's dumped you –"

"Liar," she said angrily. "He hasn't! He wrote to me only yesterday."

"Oh? So where's the letter, then?"

She went red. "At home."

"Yeah, yeah. We believe you – don't we?" I looked to the others to back me up, but none of them seemed to be on my side. "Go on, admit it. There isn't any letter. He hasn't written to you for ages."

"And you," she said, "why don't *you* admit it? There isn't any boyfriend. You made him up."

"She thought we'd be impressed," said Lucy.

"She always has to go one better than anybody else," Caroline said. "Amy had a boyfriend – so Alexa had to have one. Pathetic!"

"Don't know why she didn't invent a better name than Darren."

"Darren, Darren, Darren, Darren. She bored us to death on the subject."

They were all against me. They all hated me. Each cruel word was like a kick in the face. I wanted to turn and run away – but that would mean they had won.

Instead, I took out the cinema tickets and waved them under Amy's nose. "Look," I said. "Two tickets. If Darren doesn't exist, then why did I buy him a ticket?"

"Because you're a lunatic," said Jessica. "Sick in the head, waiting around for Mr Wonderful who's never going to arrive."

Amy laughed. "Oh, so *you* bought the tickets? What is he, your toy boy?"

"He's probably half her age. Six," said Caroline.

Lucy said, "It's past his bedtime, that's why he never showed up."

"Yeah, his mummy wouldn't let him out."

I looked down the street, half-hoping Darren would suddenly appear, half-dreading it. If they met him – the real Darren, not the boy I'd described – they would laugh even more.

But the dark street was empty. It was half past seven.

"You're missing the start of the film," I said.

"We don't care," said Caroline. "This is far more exciting. Oh, the suspense! Will he turn up or won't he?"

"I bet he doesn't," said Amy. "I bet he's not going to show. Any takers?"

Suddenly I had an awful thought. Darren had made a bet with Macaulay that he could get me to go out with him. Was that the only reason he'd asked me?

He didn't like me… not really. He didn't want to go out with me, he only did it to win money. That was all he cared about. And then, knowing he'd won the bet, he didn't even turn up! He didn't care that he'd made me look a total idiot. He was probably laughing about it right now.

At once I set off for home. Even then I didn't run, but I was walking as fast as I could. I would kill him! I would never forgive him, never! Somehow or other I would get my own back.

"You're not giving up on him, are you?" Caroline called.

"Poor Darren. You'll break his heart," cried Amy. "You don't deserve a boy like him."

"If we see him we'll give him your love."

"Kiss kiss! Ooh Darren!"

Their laughter echoed along the empty street. I never answered, I never turned my head. I didn't want them to see the tears in my eyes.

Chapter 15

Turned over

Coming into Fountain Square, I slowed down. What if Grandmother was home by now? If she saw my tear-streaked face, she would want to know what had happened.

But I could see from across the square that she wasn't home yet. There were no lights on; the windows were dark. Except... what was that?

Just for a second I had seen a blink of light. It shone through the narrow gap where my bedroom curtains didn't quite meet. It almost looked like a flash of torch-light.

I told myself I must have imagined it. But no – there it went again. There was someone in my room! Someone who shouldn't be there... a burglar?

For an instant I felt paralyzed with shock. What should I do? Find a phone... call the police... 999... I couldn't think where the nearest call-box would be. Perhaps in the hotel across the square.

Oh *do* something! Quickly!

Just then I heard a voice I knew. It was Neddy. He and Ben were leaving Ben's house – I raced towards them. I had never before been so glad to see Neddy.

"There's somebody in our house! Look – I saw a light at my window. Like someone was in there with a torch."

"Where?" said Neddy in a disbelieving voice. "I can't see anything."

We stared across at the darkened house.

"This is another of your stupid little games, isn't it?" he said. "I do wish you'd grow up a bit, Alexa. You've got a mental age of about eight." His voice stopped abruptly. We had all seen it – a small, moving light in the room above mine.

"That's my lab!" he cried. "Stop them!"

He set off at a run. Ben raced after him and grabbed his arm. "Don't be silly. Too dangerous," he hissed. "Ring the police from my house."

Ben's mother, Mrs Carson, opened the door to us. The three of us all tried to tell her at once. I thought she might not believe what we'd seen – but of course the whole Square knew about the earlier break-in. She quickly dialled 999 and explained what was happening.

"Please tell them to hurry," she said. "We think the burglars are still in the house."

It seemed an age, although it was only minutes, before the police car roared up. Two policemen ran up the steps to Grandmother's door. We hurried over with a key so that they wouldn't have to break the door down.

They went into the dark hallway. Ben's mum wouldn't let us follow them. We waited in the street, seeing lights go on all over the house, and waiting for... what? Shouts? Gunfire? I'd seen this sort of thing hundreds of times on TV. But never in real life – never in my home.

Neddy leaned over the railings to look down at the basement windows. "All shut," he said. "I wonder where they got in?"

"If they *did* get in," I said uneasily. I was beginning to think we had imagined the whole thing.

At last one of the policemen came out again. "The place has been turned over all right," he said. "But they've gone. There's a basement window open at the back…"

Neddy groaned. "I *told* Grandmother we ought to fit locks at the back."

"Can we go in?" I asked. "I want to see what's missing."

"As long as you don't touch anything," the policeman said.

Neddy ran up the stairs two at a time. I followed more slowly. I couldn't remember if I'd hidden my jewel case before I left the house. I had a dreadful feeling that I might have left it open on my dressing-table.

My room was a mess. Cupboards were open, drawers had been emptied onto the floor. And my jewellery box had definitely gone. It wasn't on the dressing-table or hidden in the fireplace.

All my nice things… my sapphire ring, great-grandmother's bracelets, my earrings and necklaces, my cameo brooch… On a normal day I would have been really upset, but tonight, strangely enough, I hardly cared. If everyone hated me, if I hadn't a single friend, then what use were rings and necklaces?

Ben's mum came in. "Oh dear," she said. "This room and your grandmother's are the worst. Have you lost much?"

"Everything," I whispered.

She didn't have a clue what I meant. But she was kind.

"It must be quite a shock," she said, putting her arm around me. "Look, you can't do anything here until the police have finished. Why don't you come home with me? You look as if you could do with a nice hot drink."

"All right," I said.

"Neddy," she called, "I'm taking Alexa home with me. I expect you can tell the police anything they need to know."

Neddy came downstairs. "Yes, of course. I'll let you know when Grandmother gets home."

"Is your lab all right?" she asked him.

He nodded. "They've taken my wallet and a few computer games, that's all."

"Computer games?" I said, surprised.

He said, "I suppose it's like Grandmother said. They take small things that are easy to sell. Hey, are you all right, Alexa?"

By now I was shivering. A glance in the mirror showed me that I looked a total wreck. My mascara had run down my cheeks; my hair was all over the place.

"She's not all right," said Ben's mum. "She's had a shock."

Too right.

Round at Ben's house, Mrs Carson gave me a drink and sat me next to a warm fire. Then she washed my face for me as if I was a baby.

"It wasn't just the burglary, was it?" she said gently. "Something happened before that. When you rang at my door, I could see you were upset... Look, you don't have to tell me if you don't want to."

I found that I was crying again. She hugged me close to her like my mother would have done – like Grandmother could never bring herself to do. (Did Grandmother dislike me too? Would Ben's mum hate me if she got to know me?)

At last the tears stopped. I had made an idiot of myself again, but I was too weary to care about that. Ben's mum asked no questions; she just waited quietly until I was ready to talk.

I said, "What would you do if you suddenly found out that no one liked you?"

For a minute she was silent. "I would be very hurt," she said. "Do you want to tell me what happened?"

I told her most of it. Not all, of course. Not Darren's name or the fact that I had been forbidden to see him. ("He's unreliable," Grandmother had said, but I thought I knew better than her. Stupid, stupid of me!)

When I had finished, Mrs Carson said thoughtfully, "It sounds to me as though you've had a lucky escape."

"What do you mean?"

"Well, if a boy doesn't care about you, it's better to find out sooner, not later. Before you really get involved. Before he breaks your heart."

Perhaps she was right – although I felt there wasn't much of my heart left unbroken.

"And those so-called friends," she went on, "I would say you're far better off without them. They sound dreadful. Do you actually *like* them?"

"Not really," I admitted. "I mean, I didn't like them much as people. I just liked being part of the gang."

"Forget them, then. Find yourself one or two good friends that you really get on with."

"But I don't know how! I keep telling you – no one likes me…"

She said, "Have you ever heard the old saying, 'The only way to have a friend is to be one'?"

I shook my head.

"What do you think that means?" she asked.

"Oh, being nice to people I suppose, and listening to them, and helping them…"

"That's right," she said. "Putting the other person first. Not going *Me, me, me* all the time."

"Has Neddy been talking about me?" I said suspiciously.

"Well, he has said a few things… But I always thought I would like to hear your side of it too. I knew you couldn't really be the monster he made you out to be." She smiled at me.

"Did he tell you I always want to win all the time? That kind of thing?"

"Something like that."

"Mum likes me to be good at things," I said. "Nice-looking. Clever. Good at sport. Good at music. So I thought that was the way to get noticed – by being the best at everything."

She said, "You were right. That *is* a good way to get noticed. But it's a hopeless way of finding friends."

While I was thinking about this, she went on, " You said no one loves you, but that isn't true, you know. There is someone who loves you."

"My parents," I said. "But they're thousands of miles away."

"Someone who loves you even more than they do."

"I suppose you mean God," I said.

"Yes. Do you believe in God?"

I hesitated. "I don't really know. Sometimes I do… sometimes not."

"The amazing thing is, even if we don't believe in him, he loves us. Whatever we're like – good or bad, clever or stupid, he loves us. He loves the winners and the losers. He wants us to love him, but even when we don't – he still loves us."

I really wished I could believe that. "How do you know?"

"This is what it says in the Bible: *Nothing can separate us from his love. Neither death nor life… neither the present nor the future… there is nothing in all creation that will ever be able to separate us from the love of God.*"

Nice words. But then I remembered what Ben had once said.

"Is it true," I said, "that God can see inside our minds?"

"Yes. He knows all about us."

I said nothing. If God knew all about *me*, knew all the bad things I'd ever done, then how could he possibly love me? Hurting Neddy, lying to Grandmother, wanting to win at all costs… God must hate me as much as everyone did.

Ben's mum seemed to guess what I was thinking.

"Let me tell you something that happened when I was little," she said. "My dad had a shed in the garden where I was never allowed to go on my own. There were sharp tools in there, and weedkiller, and things. One day when Dad was out at work, I wanted to fly my kite. I could see it, up on a shelf in the shed. I thought it wouldn't matter if, just once, I went in. Who would ever know?

"But while I was climbing up to get my kite, I knocked a big pot of paint off the shelf, and the lid came off. There was a huge great puddle of blue paint all over the floor.

"I was really petrified. I thought Dad would kill me. I tried to clean the mess up but I only made things worse. There was paint all over my hands and my shoes. And it wouldn't come off! I washed and washed my hands, but it was gloss paint, and water couldn't shift it."

"What did you do?"

"Went and hid in the bushes at the bottom of the garden. I was planning to run away as soon as it got dark – I was only about six. Then I heard Dad calling my name."

"I suppose he saw what you'd done," I said.

"Of course. He even knew where I was – there was a line of little blue footprints all down the garden. But he didn't come and drag me out. He just called my name and then waited.

"In the end I came out of my hiding-place. I told him I was really, really sorry. He must have seen by my face how upset I was, and how scared. So he didn't go mad at me. He was my dad and he loved me. Together we cleared up the mess in the shed, and then he cleaned the paint off my hands with white spirit. Soon my hands were as clean as if nothing had ever happened.

"You know, God loves us even more than my dad loved me. If we are sorry for the wrong we've done, and we come back to God, he does something quite amazing. He forgives us. He makes us clean again. To him, we become like a new-born baby who's never done anything wrong."

She stopped talking. There was a silence in the room, apart from the purr of a cat which had climbed onto my knee.

At last I said, "I would like that. But I'm not sure what to do."

"It's not difficult. You just speak to God, aloud if you like, or quietly inside your mind. Tell him that you're sorry for whatever you've done that's wrong."

So I did it. I added a silent prayer, "Please God, help me to believe in you, because I'm not even sure you exist... Are you really there?"

I don't know what I expected to hear – some kind of voice? There was nothing like that. In the room, nothing changed at all. The cat still purred on my knee, the fire still flickered. But inside me, something was different.

A great calmness came into me, like the stillness after a storm. For there had been a storm inside me – but now the raging winds became a gentle breeze. The rough sea became smooth and calm as a lake. For the first time in ages, I felt at peace.

Chapter 16

Make him pay

By the following afternoon, the house was back to normal, more or less. The fingerprint experts had been and gone. On the basement window-frame they had found clear prints, which didn't match with Grandmother's or Neddy's or mine. (We all had to have our fingerprints taken to make sure.)

"Does this mean the robbers will get caught?" I asked.

"Only if they've already got a criminal record," said Neddy. "If they've never been caught before, the police won't have their fingerprints on file."

Neddy was doing a temporary repair job on the basement window. It looked as if someone had attacked it with a chisel, hacking lumps out of the frame.

"What a mess," he said disgustedly. "The James's burglars did a far neater job. But those were professionals, the policeman said."

"What do you mean? Are there two different robbers going around?"

"That's what the police think. The ones who broke into our house probably got the idea from the other burglary. And they weren't very smart. They botched the break-in, they didn't wear gloves, they didn't nick Grandmother's credit card or your bank book. The copper said they were probably just teenagers."

"Teenagers? But why would they do it?"

"To get money for drugs. That's the usual reason, the policeman said."

"Well, they didn't get much actual money." They had found Neddy's wallet, with three pounds in it, and my purse, with thirty. The main loss was jewellery – Grandmother's and mine.

We had to make a list of the stolen items to claim on the insurance. The thing that Grandmother was saddest to lose was a silver watch. (It had belonged to my grandfather, who died long ago.) There were lots of things that I would miss, but I knew there was no point in fussing about them.

"I must say you're coping very well with this, Alexa," said Grandmother. "I thought you would have been more upset."

"What would be the use? Crying wouldn't bring my things back," I said.

"Indeed it wouldn't. But that's quite a mature attitude for someone of your age."

That strange, calm feeling was still with me. It was not something I could have created for myself; it came from somewhere outside me. From God?

When I thought about Friday night, though, I still felt angry and sore. So I tried not to think about it. At least I wouldn't have to see Amy and company on Monday – it was half-term week.

Grandmother went shopping for security locks to put on the rear windows. "Better late than never, I suppose," she said. I went down to the basement, where Neddy was still working on the window.

"How are you getting on?"

"Nearly finished," he said. "The thing that puzzles me is, how did the burglar get here?"

"Climbed over the garden wall, obviously."

"I mean before that. He would have to have come out of a house, either in Fountain Square or Pump Street. But there haven't been any more break-ins as far as we know. So – maybe it was someone local."

"Somebody you know?" I said. "What a horrible idea."

Neddy said, "There are one or two rather dodgy characters living in Pump Street." He pointed to the terraced houses that rose up beyond our back garden wall. We were looking at the backs of them – not a pretty sight. Most of them had seen better days. The most decrepit house, with a broken window and a rusty fire-escape, had a brand new satellite dish on the roof.

"That's Macaulay's house," Neddy said. "If he climbed over a couple of walls, he could easily get in here."

I said, "Do you mean Darren's friend? It wasn't him. He was in the cinema last night – I saw him go in."

"His big brother, then. He's even worse than Macaulay. I wonder if there's any clues to where they climbed over? Loose bricks, broken twigs, that kind of thing…"

"Didn't the police think of that?" I said.

"They did have a look outside, but it was pretty dark. I wouldn't be surprised if they missed something."

The small back garden was just a square of lawn, surrounded by shrubs and bushes. Some of these were very prickly, a better defence than the wall beyond. We searched all along the back border, but found nothing. Then we tried the side.

"Hey, look at this!"

Neddy showed me a bush where a couple of branches had been broken off. In the ground beneath was a dent which could have been a footprint. It was difficult to tell; the ground was very hard.

Suddenly something caught my eye – a glint of gold. It was deep in the bushes. Carefully I parted the prickly branches.

"Neddy. Look."

"Ah! That proves my theory. He got in this way, and he dropped something as he was leaving. Elementary, my dear Watson. What is it?"

He reached in and pulled out the golden thing.

"My dragon!" I cried.

The chain was broken, but the little dragon wasn't even scratched. It gazed up at me with its ruby-red eye.

"Oh well, at least you got one of your treasures back," said Neddy.

"But this one wasn't stolen," I said, puzzled. "It wasn't in my jewel case – Darren had it. The last time I saw him he was wearing it."

"What?"

We stared at each other.

"Darren," said Neddy. "So it was him!"

"The pig. Oh, the absolute pig!"

Neddy said, "He climbed over from the back yard of the café. He'd have to cross a couple of gardens – but it was dark. No one saw him."

I said, "How did he know there was no one at home? I suppose because all the lights were out. He broke in –"

"Wait a minute," said Neddy. "I can't believe Darren would actually do that. Maybe there's some other explanation."

"Explain *this* then." I held out the dragon. "How did it get into our garden?"

"Darren could have sold it to someone else. Or chucked it over the wall. This doesn't actually prove anything… I mean, it's only your word against his. He could deny that you ever gave him the thing in the first place."

"So what are we going to do? Simply let him get away with it?"

"Of course not. If we gave his name to the police, they could check his fingerprints against the ones from the window. But I don't want to do that – not unless we really have to. I want to talk to him first."

I thought this was a stupid idea. It would only give Darren warning that we were on his track. I wanted to go straight to the police. I wanted to see him get into deep, deep trouble, so deep that he would sink without trace.

But Neddy said, "Look, I've known him for a long time. I suppose he's a friend – sort of. Just give me ten minutes with him."

"Oh, all right. In any case, we can't do much until Grandmother gets back."

He went round to the café. I waited at home, getting angrier and angrier. It was unbelievable, what Darren had done. Pretending to like me, asking me out, while all the time planning to rob me. Sending Macaulay with a message, so that I would hang around the cinema for ages and ages. Stealing my things and laughing to himself. "Silly little girl, believe anything, she would…"

But now he was in my power. Now I would make him pay. I would tell the police and he would be punished. He would have a criminal record at the age of thirteen, and he would be sorry we'd ever met.

At last I heard Neddy come back.

"Look what I've got!" he said. He had a Tesco carrier bag which he emptied onto the table. Out fell my jewels, his wallet, the silver watch, four computer games…

"It's all here," he said. "Every last thing. I promised we wouldn't go to the police if he gave it all back."

"You promised *what*?"

"That we wouldn't tell the police. Do you know why he did it? His dad's in debt, his mum's expecting a baby any day now, and they're going to –"

"I know, I know. They're going to be kicked out on the street. But so what? I hope he *does* get thrown out on the street. He deserves it."

Neddy looked quite shocked at the fury in my voice.

I said, "You don't know what he did. You don't know half of it. Oh yes, he tells a good story. He makes you feel quite sorry for him, doesn't he? But it's all an act. He's only out for what he can get. He thought I was rich and I would give him money, but I didn't, so he decided to steal it instead. I hate him!"

"Look, it wasn't even his idea," said Neddy. "Macaulay talked him into it. Darren wouldn't have done it if he hadn't been desperate, and he's really sorry…"

"Good. He's going to be even sorrier when I go to the police."

"No!" Neddy cried. "That's not fair! I promised, if he gave it all back –"

"*You* may have promised that. I certainly didn't."

By now I was so wild with anger that I could not stand still. I marched out of the house. Darren was going to hear exactly what I thought of him! Sorry, oh yes – he'd be sorry all right.

Ignoring my promise to Grandmother, I ran to the café. It was busier than usual, about half-full. Several people turned to stare as I marched in. Behind the counter was a girl who must be Darren's kid sister.

"Where's Darren?" I demanded.

"Gone out," she said. "You just missed him."

"You can give him a message, then. Tell him Alexa isn't as soft as Neddy. Alexa is going to the police. Got that?"

She nodded. The word *police* had brought a frightened look to her face.

I turned towards the staring customers. In a good, loud voice, I said, "A word of warning. While you're in here, it would be wise to keep an eye on your money. There's a thief about. His name is Darren Wheeler."

Then I went out. I was smiling.

Chapter 17

Gone missing

"Have you heard about Darren? He's gone missing!"

It was Ben who told us. (Ben's sister and Darren's were friends.) Darren had not been seen since seven o'clock the previous night. His money and some of his clothes were missing, along with some food from the café. No one knew where he had gone.

"This is your fault, Alexa," said Neddy. "He was scared of being arrested, so he's gone on the run."

"*My* fault? Yours, you mean. You were the one who let him know we were onto him."

"Never mind whose fault it is," said Ben. "He's gone. His parents are really worried. His mum spent all day looking for him, asking at the station if anybody saw him, and under the pier where people sleep rough. But no luck."

Three or four days went by. Suddenly Darren's face seemed to be everywhere. His parents had got posters printed, to stick on lamp-posts and shop windows. "HAVE YOU SEEN THIS BOY? MISSING SINCE OCTOBER 26."

"I don't know why they're looking for him around here," I said. "He's probably in London. That's where

I would go if I was running away."

"But you need money to survive in London," said Neddy, "and he didn't have much. If it was me, I'd go somewhere wild and lonely, like the Scottish Highlands, and live on what I could find. Go fishing, snare rabbits, collect nuts and berries…"

"You'd starve in a week," I said scornfully.

Was Darren starving? I imagined him, hungry, cold and lonely, sitting huddled in a shop doorway somewhere. All his money was spent. He was tortured by the smell of food which he couldn't afford to buy. He longed to come home but he was too frightened.

I enjoyed this thought. It was about the only thing I *did* enjoy, because otherwise I was feeling quite miserable. The calm that had come over me a few days before had vanished now. I felt as if I was being tossed about by a storm of rage and guilt.

That was stupid, I told myself. What had *I* done wrong? Darren was the one who should feel guilty, not me. I thought of what he'd done – and once again the storm rose up inside me.

I went for a walk along the sea-front, to get out of the house and away from my thoughts. But the thoughts followed me, and Darren's face gazed out at me from every stall and lamp-post.

A high wind was getting up; enormous black clouds, low and threatening like bomber planes, were racing in from the sea. There was absolutely no one on the beach. I remembered the day I'd seen Darren with his metal-detector. The high tide, the climb up the cliff –

I stopped in my tracks. I had remembered something else – the cave.

That was where he had gone! Suddenly I was sure

of it. Hadn't he said it would make a good hideout? "You could live here, and no one would ever know…"

"Alexa!" A small car had pulled up beside me. Ben's mum was in it. "Would you like a lift home? It's going to pour down, any minute."

"Yes please."

She smiled at me as I got in. "How's things?"

"Oh, all right."

"Are you sure? I saw you walking along, and I thought, that girl's got all the cares of the world on her shoulders."

Part of me wanted to talk to her. Part of me wanted to tell her to mind her own business.

I said, "I was thinking about Darren."

"Still angry with him?"

I nodded.

"Well, that's only natural. But don't let it take over your life, will you?"

I looked at her, startled. How did she know the way I felt?

"It *is* taking over my life," I said in a low voice. "I can't stop thinking about him. Hating him. Hoping he's having a really bad time."

As we drove along, a burst of rain hit the windscreen so hard that it sounded like hail. Wind and rain seemed to attack the little car and rock it on its wheels. The storm was coming in from the sea; with any luck it would blow right into the mouth of the cave. No dry place, no shelter, no warmth…

She said, "The problem with hating someone is, it doesn't hurt him – it only hurts you. It can eat away inside you like rot inside a tooth. You can't feel close to God while you're hating someone else."

I stared out of the window.

"Jesus told a story," she said, "about two men who got into debt. Steve owed Jack ten pounds, but Jack owed his boss a thousand pounds. When the boss called him in and asked for the money, Jack knew he couldn't pay him back, even if he sold everything he had. He begged and pleaded. At last his boss said, 'I forgive you. You needn't pay. I'll forget that you ever owed me anything.' So Jack went out, feeling really happy.

"Then he bumped into Steve, who owed him just ten pounds. What do you think he did?"

"Forgave him? Let him off?"

"No. He shouted, 'Where's my money? Give it back at once!' And Steve said, 'Please – I can't pay you today, but I will, as soon as I can.' But Jack wouldn't listen. 'I won't let you off! Give me the money or I'll have you put in prison!'"

"But that was so unfair," I said. "His boss let him off far more than that."

"Exactly," she said. "And God forgives *us* a huge amount – all the wrong we've ever done in our lives. If we don't forgive other people, we're behaving like Jack. Jesus said that if we don't forgive other people, then God won't forgive us…"

I didn't want to hear any more. Luckily we were nearly home. As soon as the car stopped, I leapt out and hurried indoors, without even thanking her for the lift.

What should I do? Should I tell Darren's parents about the cave? Should I tell the police? Or should I do nothing at all?

In the end I did nothing for two days – partly because the storm kept everyone indoors, and partly because I wasn't sure I could remember exactly where the cave was. I would look a real idiot, babbling on about a mysterious cave which no one could find. Or if they did find it, Darren might not be there at all.

For two days the storm battered the town. In Pump Street three chimney-pots blew down; one of them landed in our garden. I listened to the wild wind and the driving rain, and wondered what it sounded like from inside the cave.

At last the storm died away. The air was cold and still. After being cooped up indoors, everyone wanted to go out. Grandmother had gone shopping, so I left her a note: *Gone for a walk towards Sheepstone. I have borrowed your binoculars, I hope you don't mind.*

I needed the binoculars because I was planning to look for the cave. (From a distance, of course. I didn't want to alert Darren if he was there.)

Ben and Neddy were outside with their bikes, pumping up Neddy's back tyre. Neddy saw the binoculars. "Hey, who said you could borrow those?"

"They're Grandmother's, not yours," I informed him.

"Going bird-watching?" he said, surprised. "I didn't think you could tell an osprey from an ostrich."

I told him to mind his own business, and walked off.

Crossing the river, I saw that the tide was still high. It would be no good trying to go along the shore, and anyway Darren might see me. Much better to walk along the cliff-top, where I could look down from above.

I followed the railway line for quite a long way;

then I went over to the edge of the cliff. Just before the ground fell away, a narrow footpath ran along the cliff-top. It gave an amazing view far out over the sea, which lay cold and grey under a sky the colour of stone.

But it was the cliff itself that interested me. I scanned it with the binoculars in both directions. Where, exactly, had we climbed up? There were so many rocky outcrops, so many steep grassy slopes, and they all looked the same.

Because of the steepening curve of the cliff face, I couldn't see the shoreline. Somewhere down there – to left, or right, or directly below – was the little bay where the tide had trapped us. And somewhere, half-way up the cliff, was the cave. Where, though?

I walked along the narrow path, looking for anything that seemed familiar. Once or twice I saw something moving far below, but the binoculars showed only seabirds and a rabbit. I was almost ready to give up and go home.

Then I noticed the railway signal. I remembered seeing it as Darren and I reached the top of the cliff. There was no other signal to be seen for a long way down the line. Now I knew I was close to the route of our climb. But still I couldn't see the cave.

There was nothing else for it – I would have to climb down a little way. I went carefully and quietly down a long, steep pitch of grass. It was slippery with rain. Once, my feet slid out from under me and I sat down with a bump.

I was looking for a rock-face with a heap of stones at the foot of it. I thought I saw it below and to my right – but no, that couldn't be the place. The pile of rocks was far too big.

Suddenly my foot slipped again, and I cried out in fright. That was a close one! I had slid to the very edge of a vertical drop.

Had anyone heard me call out? I lay quite still, holding my breath. I could hear the rattle of pebbles rolling down the cliff, the sigh of waves far below… and something else.

It was a voice, faint and weak, from somewhere beneath me.

"Help!" it was calling. "Help!"

Chapter 18

Falling rocks

"Darren?" I shouted. "Is that you? Where are you?"

"I'm here. In the cave."

Strange – I couldn't see any cave. Looking over the edge of the steep drop in front of me, all I could see was a big pile of rocks. By going a long way to one side, I managed to climb down and round the steep place. Now I was on a level with the heap of stones, which was taller than I was.

"Where are you?" I called again.

"In the cave. The roof fell in and I can't get out."

His voice came from somewhere behind the rocks. I began to try to move them, but most of them were enormously heavy.

"I can't possibly do this on my own," I gasped. "I'll have to fetch help. Are you hurt?"

"No. I was dead lucky, I was right at the back when it fell. But there's not much food left… or water."

"When did it happen? How long have you been trapped?"

"I dunno. Two days? Three days? It's so dark in here…" His voice sounded shaky. "Boy, am I glad you're here, Alexa. I thought you must have forgotten about this place. I thought nobody would ever find me."

Suddenly I remembered – this was *Darren* I was talking to.

"Glad I'm here? That makes a change," I said coldly.

There was a silence.

"Look, about last Friday," he said, "I'm really sorry. I wouldn't have done it, except I was desperate, and Macaulay said you wouldn't care, you'd get it all back on the insurance…"

"I'm not talking about the burglary," I snapped. "I'm talking about the way you stood me up. All my friends – all the others were laughing at me."

"I didn't mean for that to happen. I thought I could do the job and still be in time to see you. But breaking in took much longer than what I thought –"

"Oh, terrific. So you'd steal my things and then get me to give you an alibi, is that what you're saying?"

"It was Macaulay's idea." He sounded uncomfortable.

"Yeah, yeah. Nothing's ever your fault. You think you can talk your way out of anything… but not this time. You can't talk your way out of that cave."

He said nothing.

"I think I'm going to leave you here," I said. "I think I'll simply walk away and forget I ever saw this place."

"No!" he cried. "No! You can't do that!"

"Oh, can't I? Give me one good reason why not."

"You can have some of the money. I'll give you a quarter of it if you get me out of here."

"Money? What money?" I said scornfully. "You haven't got any."

"Not *my* money. Well, it's mine now – I found it.

It's gold, Alexa! It was hidden in the cave."

"You're making this up," I said.

"No, I'm not, I swear to God. See, when that storm came up, the rain was blowing right in. So I started digging at the side, making the cave bigger so I could keep dry. It's not all rock – some of it is clay sort of stuff. I could dig it out quite easy with a stone."

"What a dumb thing to do," I said. "That's probably what made the roof fall in."

"Could be. But that's how I found the money."

"What money?" I said again.

"Gold coins. At least I think they're gold – forty-three of them. And a few silver ones too. Really old, they are. All buried in the wall of the cave, wrapped up in a bit of old rag. If you get me out of here, I'll give you… I'll give you half of it."

I began to laugh.

"What's so funny?"

"You! All you care about is money, and now you've got it, it's not doing you any good. You can't eat it. You can't drink it. It won't help you get out of the cave."

"Three-quarters," he said desperately. "You can have three-quarters of the money if you help me! Please, Alexa!"

"Don't you see? I intend to have *all* of it, and you can't stop me. I'm going home now. I'll be back in a few weeks, but there won't be much left of you by then. A few bones, probably, that's all… and the money, of course."

"No!" he screamed. "No! Come back! You can keep it all, all the money. Just get me out of here!"

"Goodbye, Darren. Sleep well."

I started climbing up the cliff. Then I had a sudden thought – would I be able to find the place again? I laid out some stones on the grass, making an arrow shape which could be seen from the cliff-top.

Of course I wasn't really going to leave Darren to die, but why tell him that? Let him panic. Let him worry about it, imprisoned in the dark. Before we came to dig him out, he would have an hour or two of total despair. Excellent!

Finders keepers, losers weepers? Not this time, Darren. More like "Finders weepers, losers winners." For I had won in the end – anyone could see that.

When I got to the top of the cliff, I stood still, wondering which way to go. Westhaven lay to the right, about two miles away. Much nearer, less than a mile to my left, I could see a row of cottages close to the cliff-top. It would be far quicker to phone for help from there – provided they were on the phone.

There was no one to help me decide; no one in sight, apart from a couple of walkers far along the cliff path. Quickly making my mind up, I turned left. Oh God, please tell me I'm doing the right thing!

But God gave no answer. I was on my own.

I hurried along the cliff-top path. No time now to look at the view, or think about anything except getting help. I was starting to think I shouldn't have said those things to Darren. The hope of being rescued had helped to keep him alive… but now that hope had been taken away. What would he do – give up? Lie down and die?

Very slowly, it seemed, the houses drew nearer. I saw that it was the place called Sheepstone, next to the railway. And yes, there was a phone line leading to the row of cottages. I ran up to the first house and banged on the door.

Nobody came. They must be out – I tried the next house. No answer there either. The next one had its curtains drawn, like a holiday cottage shut up for the winter. No answer at the next house, or the next. And now I saw there were no cars parked outside any of them.

Just my luck! I would have to go all the way back to Westhaven, or on towards Barcliff. And already I'd wasted so much time… But wait a minute. Maybe I could still use the phone – by breaking in. After all, it was an emergency.

Perhaps I could use Neddy's trick of opening a window catch. A knife – I needed a knife or a screwdriver. I ran around the back of the house, looking for a shed which might have tools in it. The back garden was neglected and weedy, but there was a shed and the door was open.

I was just going in when I heard a train coming. For a moment I hesitated. Should I run back towards the railway, and somehow signal to the driver? Wave, or something?

No, there wasn't time. Already the train was so close that the noise of it seemed to shake the ground. Those cottages must be awful to live in, with every passing train making your teeth rattle. Even after the train had gone by, the earth still seemed to tremble.

What was happening? Instead of dying away, the shaking grew worse. I clutched the door of the shed. I saw a jagged crack open up in the earth below, like a huge brown mouth yawning.

And then the shed, and myself, and half the garden, all tilted sideways and slid slowly down the cliff.

Chapter 19

Roller-coaster

It was like the moment when the roller-coaster seems to hang over the drop. Then it falls, slowly at first – and then faster, faster… I closed my eyes and screamed.

All at once came a shuddering jolt. The ground seemed to come up and hit me. In my ears was a vast, thundering roar, far louder than the train.

But I seemed to have stopped moving. I found I could open my eyes – still alive, then. I was lying on my back looking up at the sky. Above me was the cliff-top, with a huge bite taken out of it. Below me… my heart almost stopped. Below me, a long way down, was the sea.

Raw earth and fallen rocks lay heaped at the foot of the cliff, like rubble tipped from a giant lorry. One false move and I would be down there too. I was on a rocky ledge not much wider than a table. It felt quite solid – at the moment.

But what would happen when another train came by? Would the roller-coaster ride begin again… this time right to the bottom?

"Help! Help!" I shrieked.

It was useless. There was no one to hear – no one for miles around. Today there was not even a ship on the far horizon. I was quite alone... trapped and helpless, just like Darren.

Fury rose up in me again. This was all Darren's fault! If he hadn't run away, if he hadn't got himself trapped in the cave, I wouldn't be here now.

If I was going to die, Darren would die too, for no one else knew where he was. But at least I would die quickly. His death would be horrible... a long, slow starvation, alone in the dark.

Oh God, help me! Help both of us!

I stared out over the empty sea. Where was God when you really needed him? Answer: he wasn't there.

I must have imagined the peace and calm that I'd felt before, and the sense of nearness to God. Because he didn't exist – there was nobody out there. The whole universe was empty and cold, like the sea.

Nothing can separate us from the love of God... Nice words. But that's all it was... only words. Ben's mum seemed to believe in it, but if ever her life was in danger, she would soon find out the truth.

All of a sudden I remembered something else that Ben's mum had said. *If we don't forgive other people, then God won't forgive us.*

Then something weird happened. It was like a dream, except that I wasn't asleep. I saw a picture in my mind – a girl hiding deep inside a cave. She could see light at the entrance to the cave, but she wouldn't go towards it. She liked the darkness better.

Was that meant to be me? Was God telling me something?

Help me! I don't understand!

Perhaps, if I chose to live in the dark – if I chose hatred and bitterness and revenge – I could never be free. I could never know the light of God's love.

So what must I do?

The answer came clearly: Stop hating Darren. Forgive him.

All right, I told God reluctantly. I forgive him. I'll try not to hate him any more. It won't be easy – but I'll try. That is, if I ever get out of this alive...

"Alexa!"

I looked up, startled. Where the cliff curved round to the east, I could see two people outlined against the sky. They had seen me; they were waving frantically.

"Don't come any closer!" I shouted. "It's not safe!"

It was Neddy and Ben. What were they doing here?

"Keep still," Neddy called. "Don't move. We'll go and get help."

"Tell them to stop the trains!"

They looked at each other as if to say, she's gone mad.

"The trains," I yelled desperately. "When the trains go past, they shake the ground –"

Neddy understood at once. "We'll tell them."

There was something else, something even more vital. "And tell them Darren's trapped in a cave. All you can see is this pile of stones. I marked it with an arrow..."

"Okay, we know where it is," Ben called. "We saw you from a long way off."

"Don't move. Don't go anywhere," Neddy shouted.

They ran off, out of sight. Soon I heard the crash of glass from somewhere above me – they were breaking into a house, and wasting no time.

The two of them appeared again along the curve of the cliff.

"They're sending a helicopter," Neddy shouted.

"A *helicopter*?"

"Yes. As soon as we mentioned Sheepstone, they didn't hang about."

Long minutes passed. At last we heard the helicopter approaching. It hovered above the cliff. I could feel the fierce down-draught of its rotors, and I understood why it did not come closer.

A man was lowered on the end of a cable. He landed smoothly beside me, helped me get up and strapped me into the harness he wore.

"Okay? You're safe now. Soon be home and dry."

He signalled to someone above. The two of us were winched up slowly, like a huge spider reeling itself up on a thread.

I looked down only once. Below were the cottage roofs, and further below, the long, long drop to the sea. I felt terrified, dizzy and sick.

Then I had to laugh, because I saw Ben and Neddy gazing up at me. On their upturned faces was a look of the purest envy.

Chapter 20

The prize

It was all in the local paper the following week.
"CLIFF RESCUE DRAMA – TWO CHILDREN
SAVED."

"They've got this all wrong," I said in disgust. "I'm
twelve, not ten. And Darren was only trapped for two
days – not a week. Who writes this stuff, anyway?"

"Don't be rude about the *Westhaven Weekly*," said
Neddy. "It helped to save your life, remember?"

In a way that was true. The previous week the paper
had reported on the people of Sheepstone being forced
to leave their homes. The storm which buffeted the
cliffs had made ominous cracks appear in the ground.
It wasn't safe to live there any longer.

I hadn't seen the news, but Ben had. When he and
Neddy saw my note to Grandmother, they realised I
could be heading into danger. That was when they
decided to go and find me.

"I bet it was Ben's idea," I said to Neddy. "I bet *you*
didn't want to."

He looked rather guilty. "Well... only because I
thought you'd be angry. You'd tell us it was none of
our business."

"I didn't, though."

"No," he said. "You were quite pleased to see us, I seem to remember."

"So it wasn't the newspaper that saved my life," I said. "It was you and Ben. Thanks, er... Edward. And look – I'm sorry I've been so awful to you."

He looked at me, astonished. I could see he couldn't quite believe what he was hearing.

"That's okay," he said at last. "And you may as well call me Neddy. Everyone else does."

"Alexa!" Grandmother called. "You have a visitor."

Who on earth? I never had visitors.

It was Darren. He stood on the doorstep looking nervous. "Got something for you," he said, and held out a small plastic bag.

I almost dropped it straight away, it was so heavy. It was full of money – old money, tarnished and dirty and smelling of the earth it had lain in.

"I said you could have it, remember?" he said. "If you got me out of the cave. And you did, so..."

"Oh, Darren! I don't want this – it's yours. You found it."

"No, no. A promise is a promise," he said, backing away.

"But I didn't mean all those things I said. I wasn't really going to leave you there, I only wanted to scare you."

"Yeah," he said. "But I was thinking, and I reckon it's unlucky, this money. I bet one of the old wreckers lifted it off a dead body. He didn't want to share it with his mates, so he hid it. But then something bad must have happened to him, or else why did he never come back for the money? Unlucky, see. And it wasn't too lucky for me either, finding it."

"So you decided to pass the bad luck on to *me*," I said. "Sweet of you, Darren."

"No! That's not what I meant. I just thought –"

At this point Grandmother decided to intervene. "May I have a look?" she asked.

When she saw the money, her eyes opened wide. "Well! I'm no expert, but a find like this could be extremely valuable. You must report it, Darren, either to the police or to a museum. If the coins are rare or historically important, you won't be allowed to keep them…"

"I don't care," said Darren.

"But you *will* receive a reward for handing them in."

"Is that right?" said Darren eagerly. "How much?"

Oh, typical! But I had stopped hating Darren. I didn't like him much, but I didn't hate him either. (Maybe I never really liked him at all; I simply liked the idea of having a boyfriend. I had been using him, just as he'd been using me.)

Grandmother said, "I believe the reward is usually equal to the value of the find. There was a case in the news quite recently, where the finder got five thousand pounds."

"Whatever the reward is," I said, "it's yours, Darren. I don't want any of it. Your family needs the money – I don't."

He gave me a grateful look. "Five thousand pounds…" he said longingly.

"But it wouldn't be enough, would it? You need ten thousand."

"Five thousand would get the bank manager off our backs for a while, though."

"Well, we must wait and see," said Grandmother. "These things do take time."

He said, "I'll go down the police station right away. Bye!"

And he hurried off, as if he was scared I would change my mind.

I really didn't want to go back to school after half-term. I thought the other girls – four against one – would make my life a misery.

But it wasn't like that. Apparently Caroline and Lucy had quarrelled during half-term. Amy was on Lucy's side, Jessica was on Caroline's, and they spent all their time making bitchy remarks about each other. For once I was quite happy to be ignored.

I've made friends with a new girl called Helen, who is much nicer than Amy and company. When they have their slanging matches – back and forth, back and forth, like an endless, exhausting game of tennis – I keep well out of the way. I can see now that no one ever wins that kind of game. Or not for long.

I think there are two ways of being a winner. One is by doing something as well as you possibly can – and there's nothing wrong with that. The other way is by trampling over other people so you can get to the top. Pushing them down so that you can climb up. And then standing at the top of the heap, shouting, "Hey, everyone! Look at me!"

When I talked to Ben's mum about this, she said, "Yes, you're right. And then there's a third way of being a winner."

"Is there?"

"This is what Jesus said to his friends, when they were arguing over which of them was the best and the greatest. *Whoever wants to be first must place himself last of all and be the servant of all.*"

"Oh." I didn't much like the sound of that.

Ben's mum laughed. "Being a servant – Jesus didn't mean scrubbing floors and washing dishes. He meant helping other people. Being ready to do what needs to be done, without complaining."

I still didn't like the sound of it. "In our house, that *does* mean washing dishes," I said gloomily. "And a whole lot of other things, too."

"Does it sound difficult? Think of it as getting into training. Nobody ever gets to be a winner without training hard... And in the end the prize will be worth it."

"What do you mean? What prize?"

"The prize of meeting with God in heaven, and hearing him say *Well done*. Because that's all that counts in the end. Some people spend their whole lives trying to win things here on earth – trying to be famous or rich or popular – but when they die, they lose it all. They've simply wasted their lives.

"But the Bible says," she went on, "each time we do something that pleases God – something kind or loving or unselfish – it's like we're storing up treasures in heaven. And those winnings will last for ever."

I'm still not sure I understand. It's all so different – so completely opposite to the way I've always lived. But if God really wants people to live like that, perhaps I should try it.

I will be nicer to Neddy – which is actually quite fun, because it shocks him so much. I will do what Grandmother says, no arguing. I will wash the dishes without being told. (Well, sometimes. Let's not get carried away.)

I'll write to my parents more often, even when I don't want money. I will stop being nasty to Lilo Green. I will try to remember that winning isn't everything in life.

Just watch me! I'm going to be so good at this – the best!